DANIEL DEFOE

ROBINSON CRUSOE

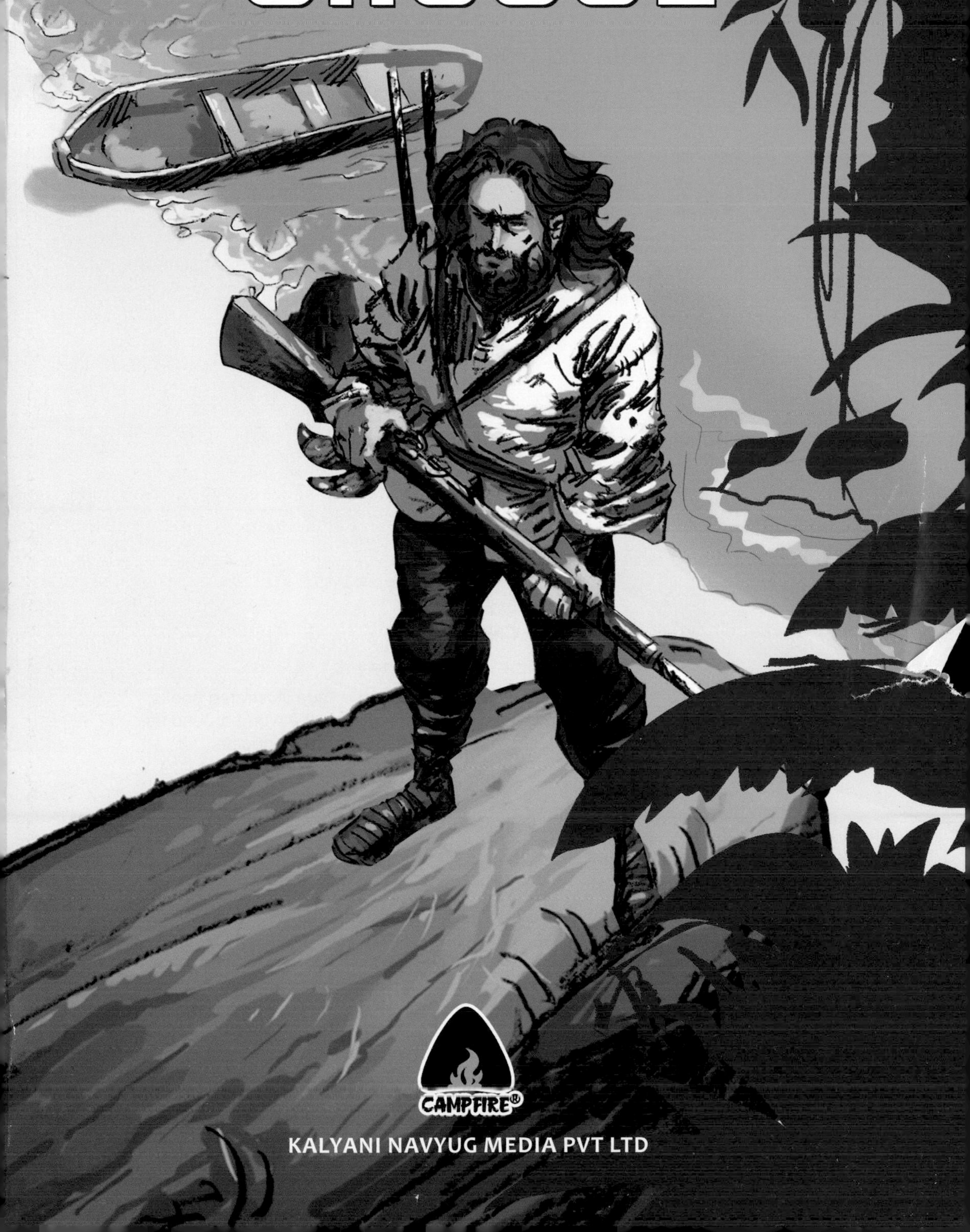

CAMPFIRE®

KALYANI NAVYUG MEDIA PVT LTD

DANIEL DEFOE
ROBINSON CRUSOE

Wordsmith	:	Dan Johnson
Illustrator	:	Naresh Kumar
Colorist	:	Anil C.K.
Letterer	:	Bhavnath Chaudhary
Editors	:	Eman Chowdhary
		Andrew Dodd
Designer	:	Vijay Sharma
Cover Designer	:	Vinay Kashyap

CAMPFIRE®

Mission Statement

To entertain and educate young minds by creating unique illustrated books
that recount stories of human values, arouse curiosity in the world around us,
and inspire with tales of great deeds of unforgettable people.

Published by Kalyani Navyug Media Pvt Ltd
101 C, Shiv House, Hari Nagar Ashram
New Delhi 110014, India

ISBN: 978-93-80028-20-0

Printed in India

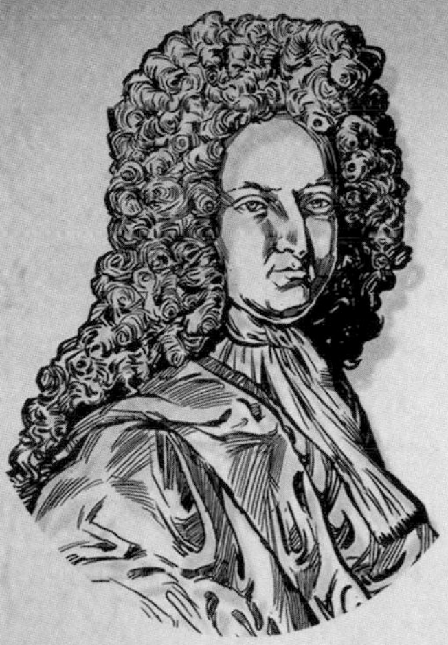

About the Author

Daniel Defoe was born in 1660 in St. Giles, London. He is most well known for his critically acclaimed novel, *Robinson Crusoe*. When published in 1719, it was instantly met with great praise. This was largely because it was a groundbreaking work—no one had produced anything like this before, and some even claim it was the first novel in English.

After finishing his schooling, Defoe was sent to Morton's Academy at Stoke Newington—an educational institute for non-conformist Christians. In 1684, he married Mary Tuffley, and had eight children in the years that followed.

Defoe faced many trials and tribulations during his life. He tried his hand in business, as well as secretarial work, but neither of these occupations worked well for him. His monetary problems are well documented—he went bankrupt in 1692—and in 1703, he was imprisoned for publishing pamphlets in support of the non-conformists.

In addition to novels and pamphlets, Defoe wrote biographies, guidebooks, journals, poems, and newspapers. In total, more than five hundred works have been attributed to his fertile mind. By far his most famous work, *Robinson Crusoe* was probably inspired by the true story of Alexander Selkirk and his experiences. Although it was not intended to be a work of fiction initially, it ended up as an adventure story, appealing to people of all ages and from all walks of life. Defoe's writing style is serious and factual, and the images he conjures up with his use of words, are vivid and realistic.

Toward the latter half of his life, he wrote under the name of Andrew Moreton, and was in hiding from his creditors when he died on April 26, 1731.

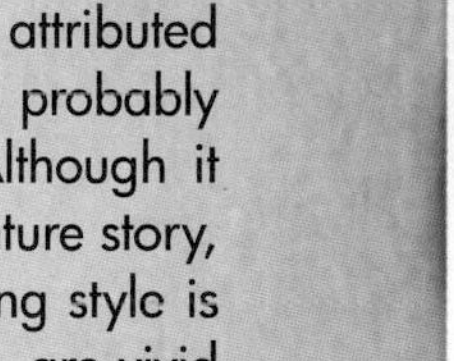

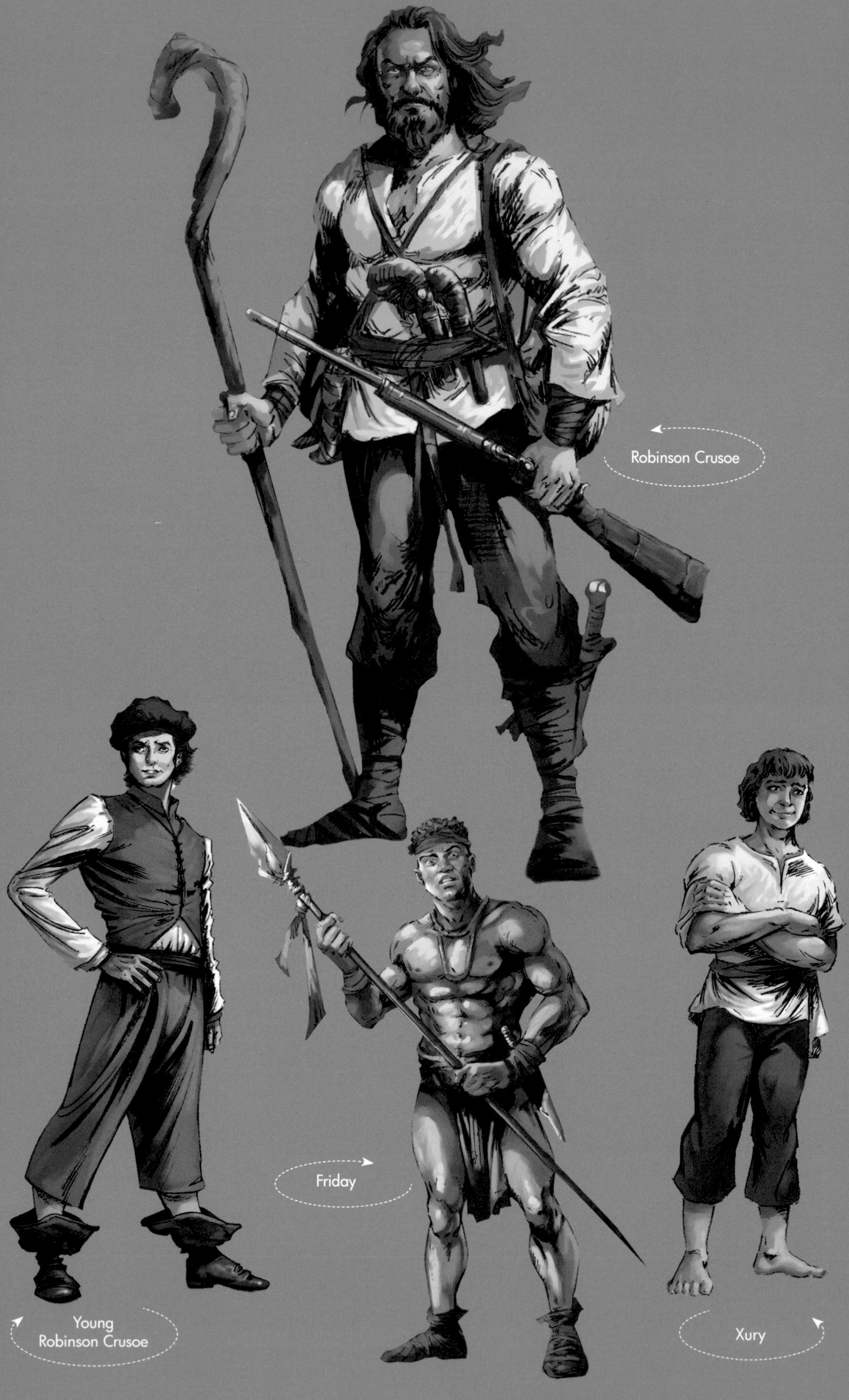
Robinson Crusoe
Young Robinson Crusoe
Friday
Xury

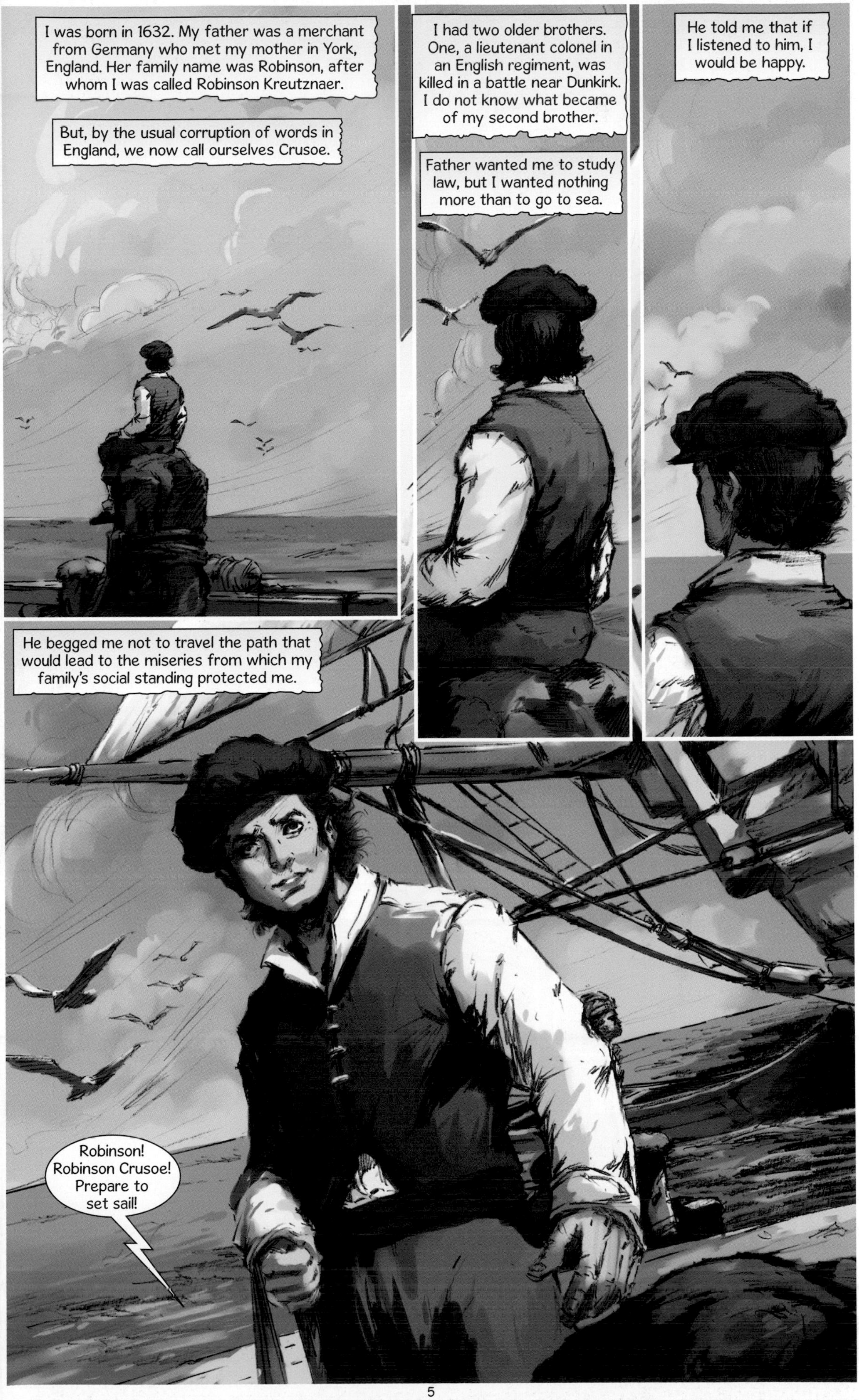
I was born in 1632. My father was a merchant from Germany who met my mother in York, England. Her family name was Robinson, after whom I was called Robinson Kreutznaer.
But, by the usual corruption of words in England, we now call ourselves Crusoe.
I had two older brothers. One, a lieutenant colonel in an English regiment, was killed in a battle near Dunkirk. I do not know what became of my second brother.
Father wanted me to study law, but I wanted nothing more than to go to sea.
He told me that if I listened to him, I would be happy.
He begged me not to travel the path that would lead to the miseries from which my family's social standing protected me.
Robinson! Robinson Crusoe! Prepare to set sail!

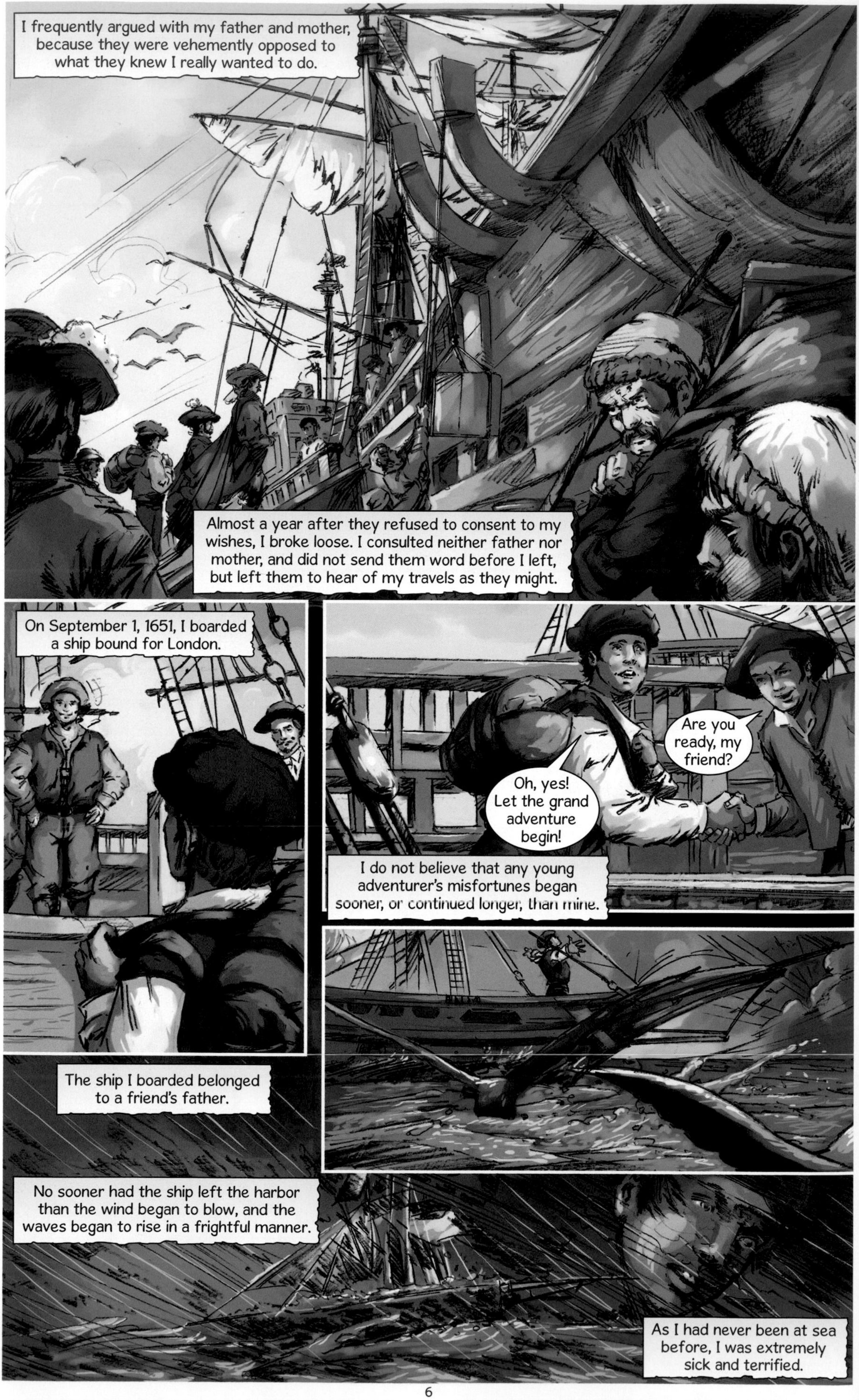
I frequently argued with my father and mother, because they were vehemently opposed to what they knew I really wanted to do.
Almost a year after they refused to consent to my wishes, I broke loose. I consulted neither father nor mother, and did not send them word before I left, but left them to hear of my travels as they might.
On September 1, 1651, I boarded a ship bound for London.
Are you ready, my friend?
Oh, yes! Let the grand adventure begin!
I do not believe that any young adventurer's misfortunes began sooner, or continued longer, than mine.
The ship I boarded belonged to a friend's father.
No sooner had the ship left the harbor than the wind began to blow, and the waves began to rise in a frightful manner.
As I had never been at sea before, I was extremely sick and terrified.

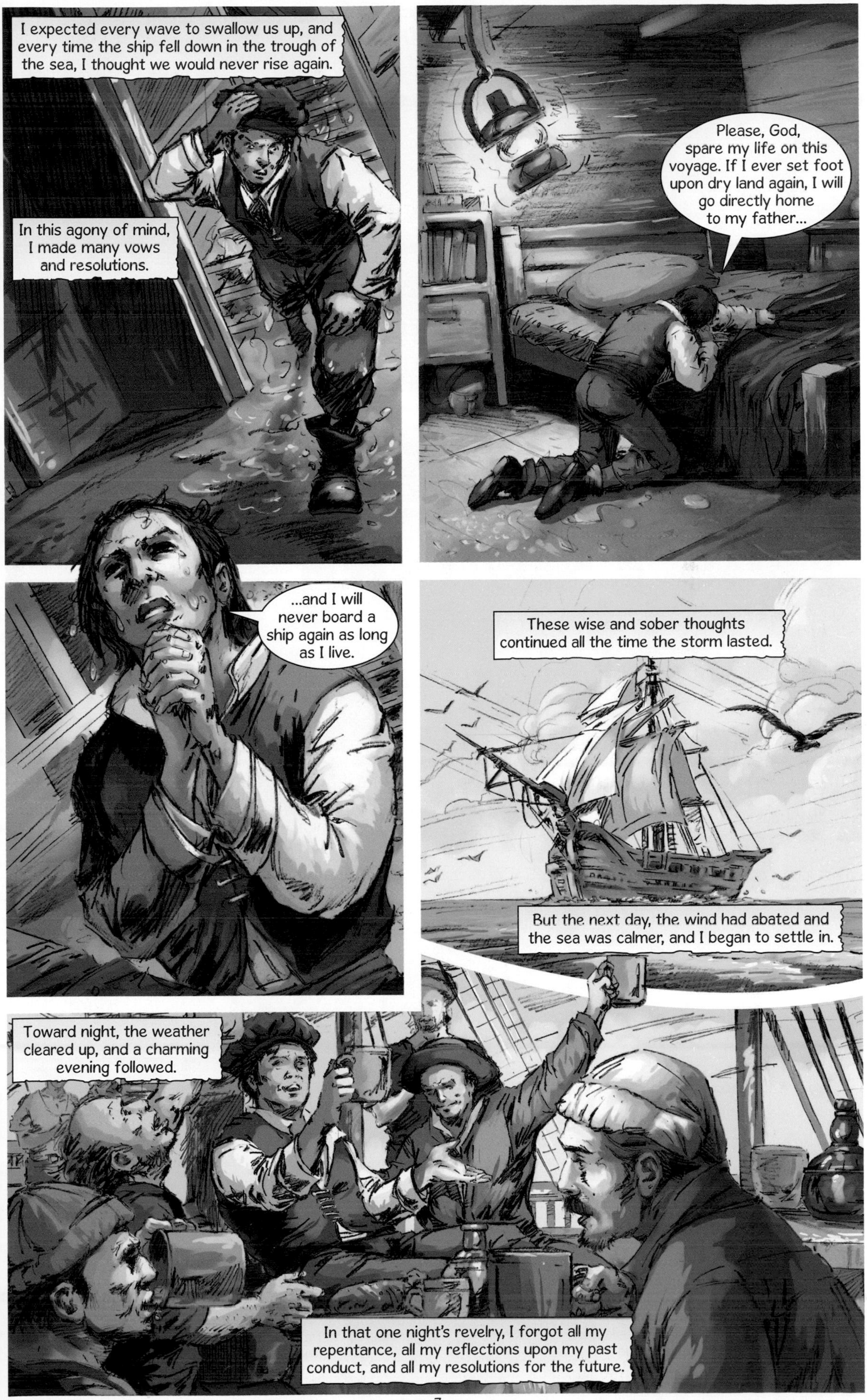
I expected every wave to swallow us up, and every time the ship fell down in the trough of the sea, I thought we would never rise again.
In this agony of mind, I made many vows and resolutions.
Please, God, spare my life on this voyage. If I ever set foot upon dry land again, I will go directly home to my father...
...and I will never board a ship again as long as I live.
These wise and sober thoughts continued all the time the storm lasted.
But the next day, the wind had abated and the sea was calmer, and I began to settle in.
Toward night, the weather cleared up, and a charming evening followed.
In that one night's revelry, I forgot all my repentance, all my reflections upon my past conduct, and all my resolutions for the future.

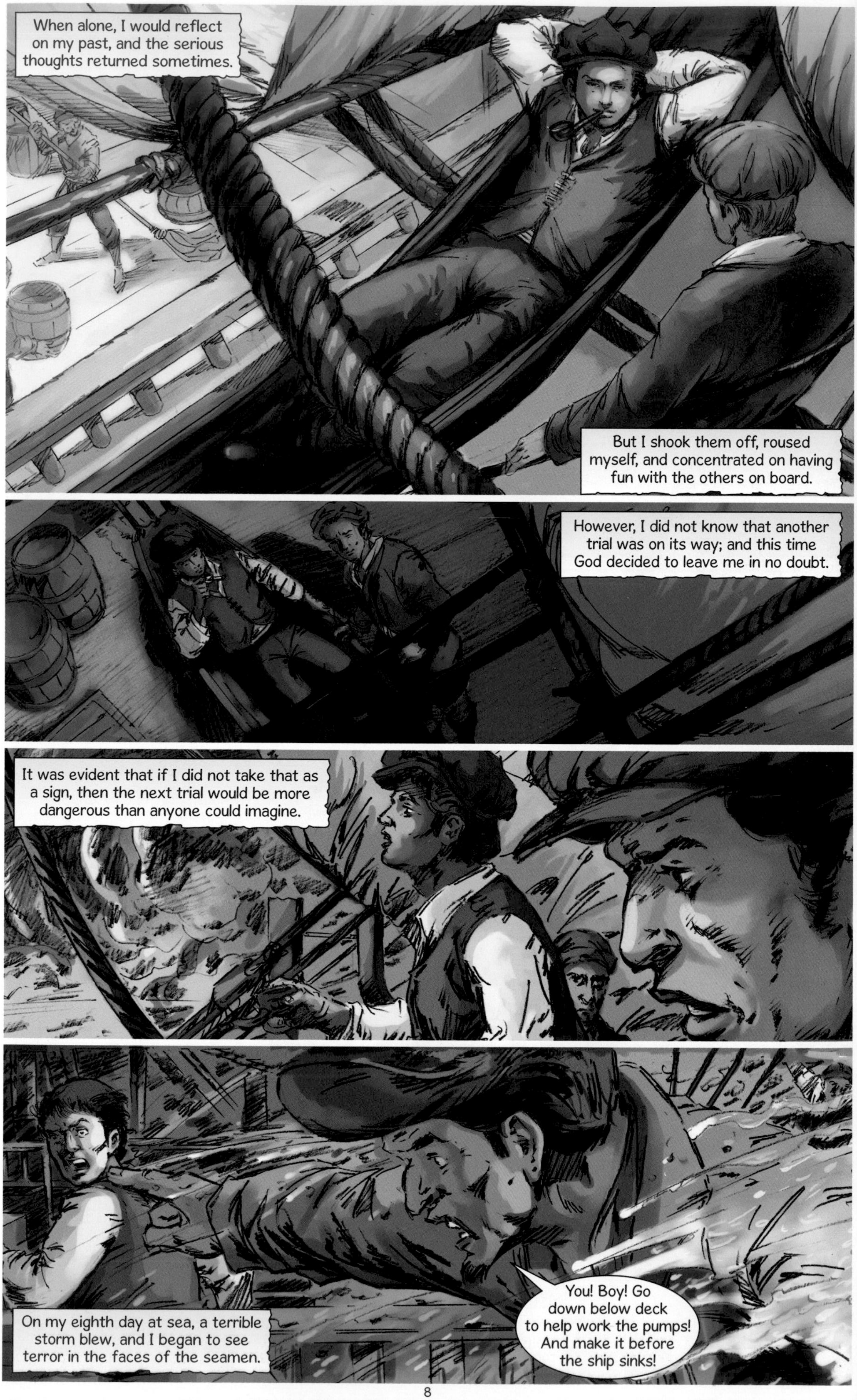
When alone, I would reflect on my past, and the serious thoughts returned sometimes.
But I shook them off, roused myself, and concentrated on having fun with the others on board.
However, I did not know that another trial was on its way; and this time God decided to leave me in no doubt.
It was evident that if I did not take that as a sign, then the next trial would be more dangerous than anyone could imagine.
On my eighth day at sea, a terrible storm blew, and I began to see terror in the faces of the seamen.
You! Boy! Go down below deck to help work the pumps! And make it before the ship sinks!

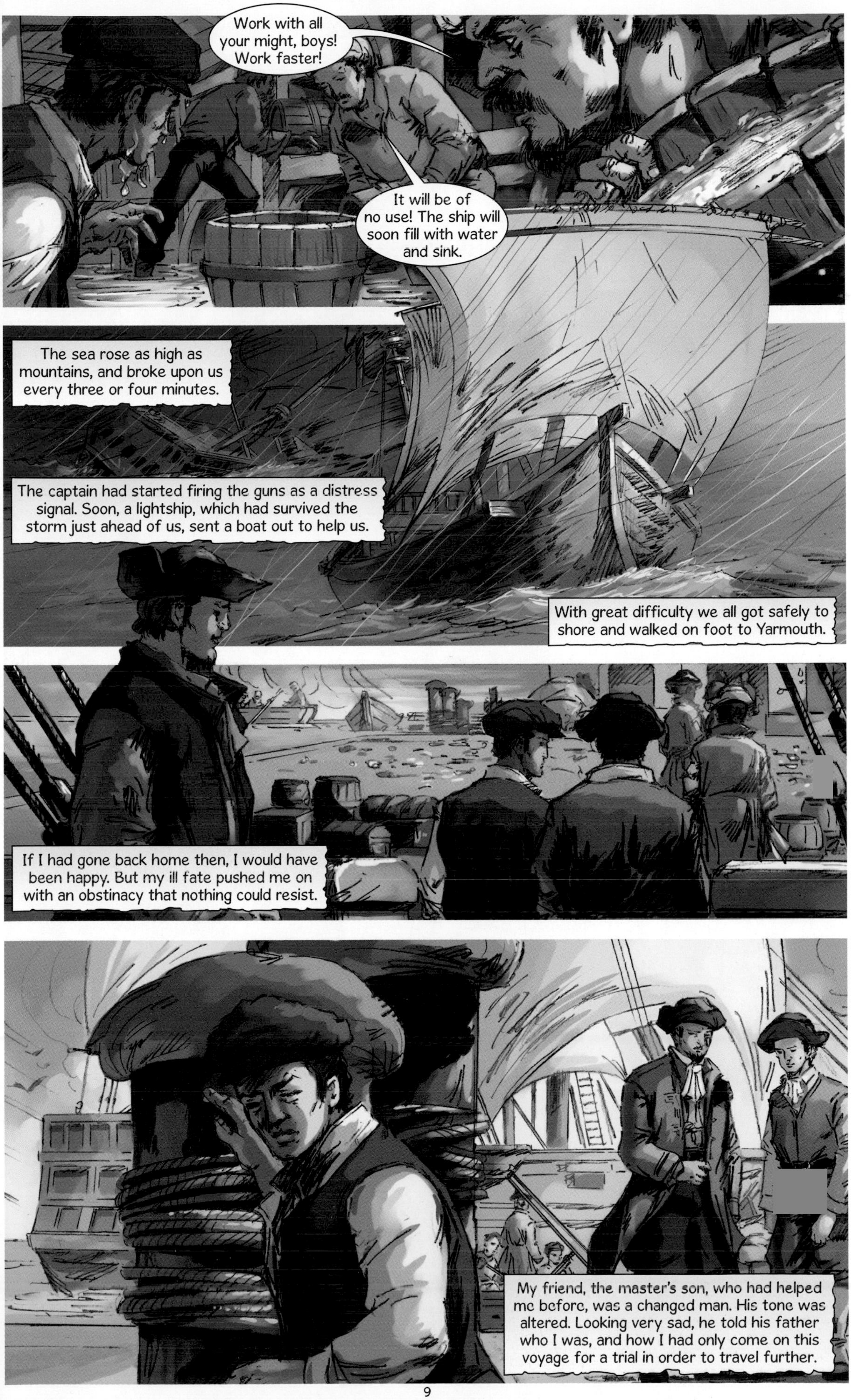
Work with all your might, boys! Work faster!
It will be of no use! The ship will soon fill with water and sink.
The sea rose as high as mountains, and broke upon us every three or four minutes.
The captain had started firing the guns as a distress signal. Soon, a lightship, which had survived the storm just ahead of us, sent a boat out to help us.
With great difficulty we all got safely to shore and walked on foot to Yarmouth.
If I had gone back home then, I would have been happy. But my ill fate pushed me on with an obstinacy that nothing could resist.
My friend, the master's son, who had helped me before, was a changed man. His tone was altered. Looking very sad, he told his father who I was, and how I had only come on this voyage for a trial in order to travel further.

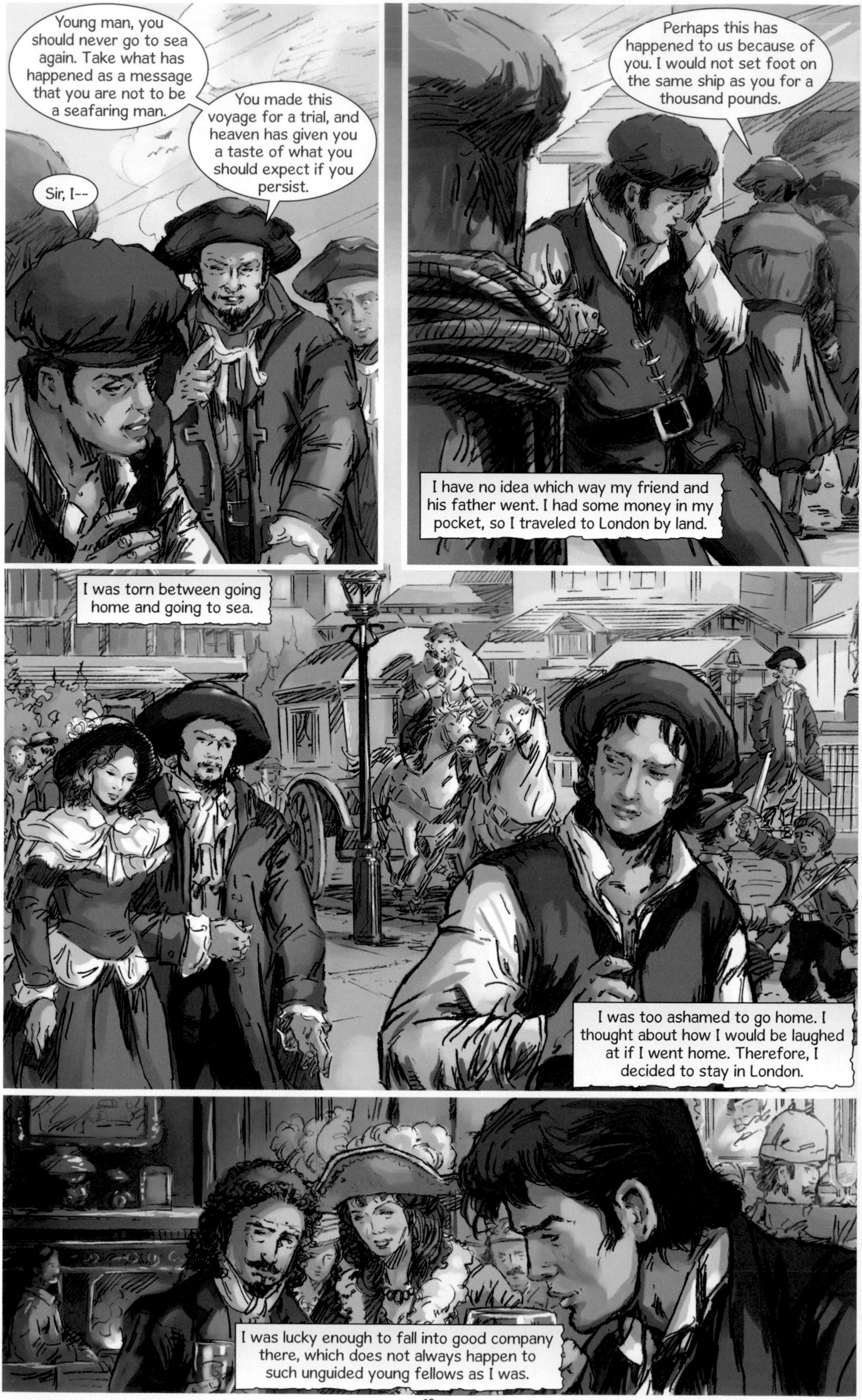
Young man, you should never go to sea again. Take what has happened as a message that you are not to be a seafaring man.
You made this voyage for a trial, and heaven has given you a taste of what you should expect if you persist.
Sir, I--
Perhaps this has happened to us because of you. I would not set foot on the same ship as you for a thousand pounds.
I have no idea which way my friend and his father went. I had some money in my pocket, so I traveled to London by land.
I was torn between going home and going to sea.
I was too ashamed to go home. I thought about how I would be laughed at if I went home. Therefore, I decided to stay in London.
I was lucky enough to fall into good company there, which does not always happen to such unguided young fellows as I was.

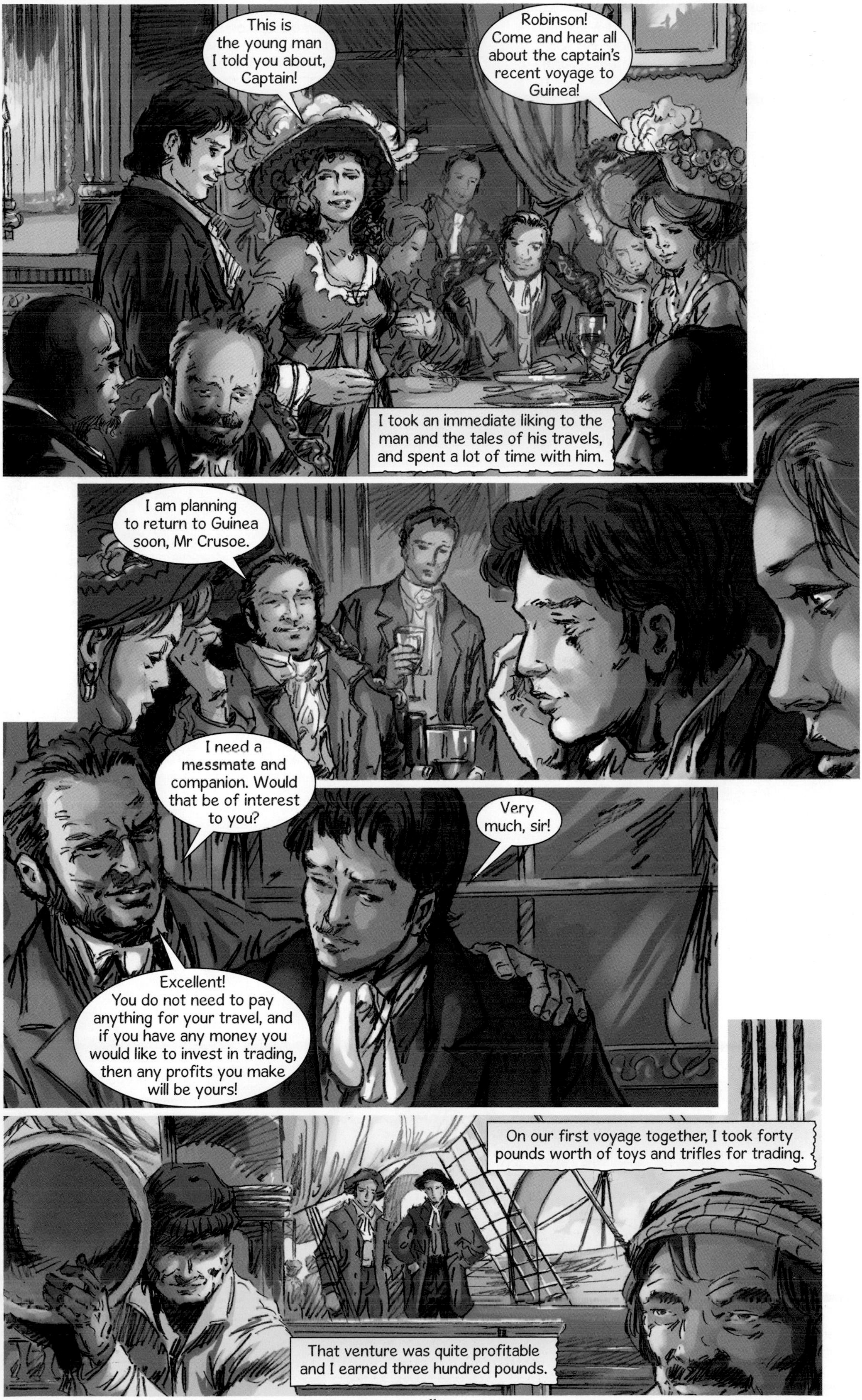
This is the young man I told you about, Captain!
Robinson! Come and hear all about the captain's recent voyage to Guinea!
I took an immediate liking to the man and the tales of his travels, and spent a lot of time with him.
I am planning to return to Guinea soon, Mr Crusoe.
I need a messmate and companion. Would that be of interest to you?
Very much, sir!
Excellent! You do not need to pay anything for your travel, and if you have any money you would like to invest in trading, then any profits you make will be yours!
On our first voyage together, I took forty pounds worth of toys and trifles for trading.
That venture was quite profitable and I earned three hundred pounds.

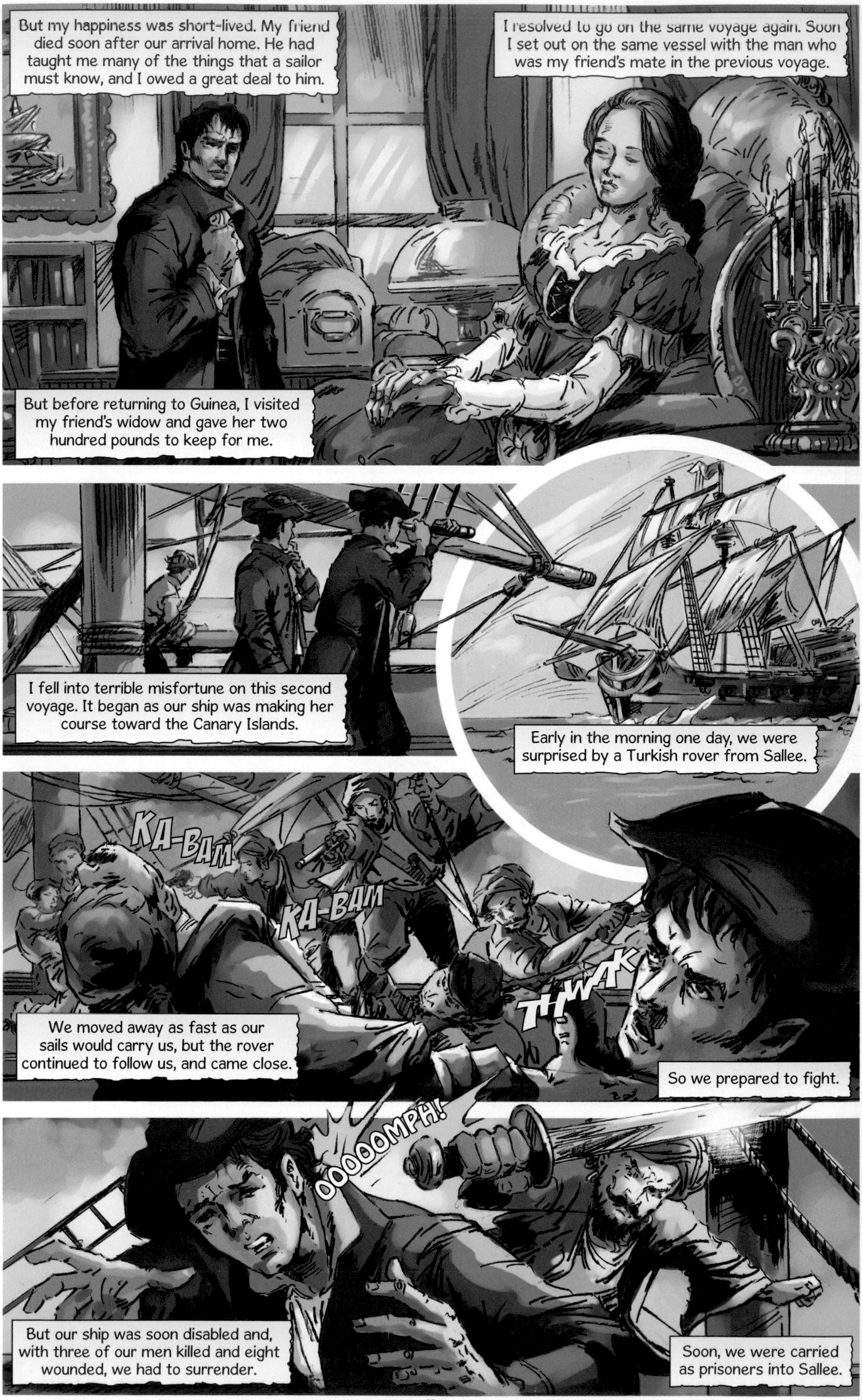

But my happiness was short-lived. My friend died soon after our arrival home. He had taught me many of the things that a sailor must know, and I owed a great deal to him.
I resolved to go on the same voyage again. Soon I set out on the same vessel with the man who was my friend's mate in the previous voyage.
But before returning to Guinea, I visited my friend's widow and gave her two hundred pounds to keep for me.
I fell into terrible misfortune on this second voyage. It began as our ship was making her course toward the Canary Islands.
Early in the morning one day, we were surprised by a Turkish rover from Sallee.
KA-BAM
KA-BAM
THWAK
We moved away as fast as our sails would carry us, but the rover continued to follow us, and came close.
So we prepared to fight.
OOOOOMPH!
But our ship was soon disabled and, with three of our men killed and eight wounded, we had to surrender.
Soon, we were carried as prisoners into Sallee.

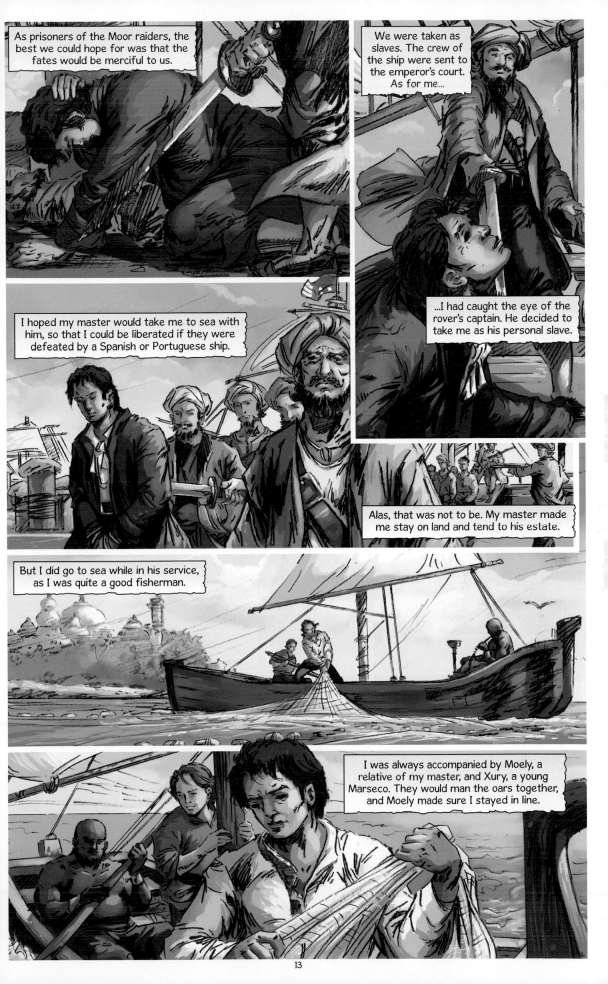

As prisoners of the Moor raiders, the best we could hope for was that the fates would be merciful to us.

We were taken as slaves. The crew of the ship were sent to the emperor's court. As for me...

...I had caught the eye of the rover's captain. He decided to take me as his personal slave.

I hoped my master would take me to sea with him, so that I could be liberated if they were defeated by a Spanish or Portuguese ship.

Alas, that was not to be. My master made me stay on land and tend to his estate.

But I did go to sea while in his service, as I was quite a good fisherman.

I was always accompanied by Moely, a relative of my master, and Xury, a young Marseco. They would man the oars together, and Moely made sure I stayed in line.

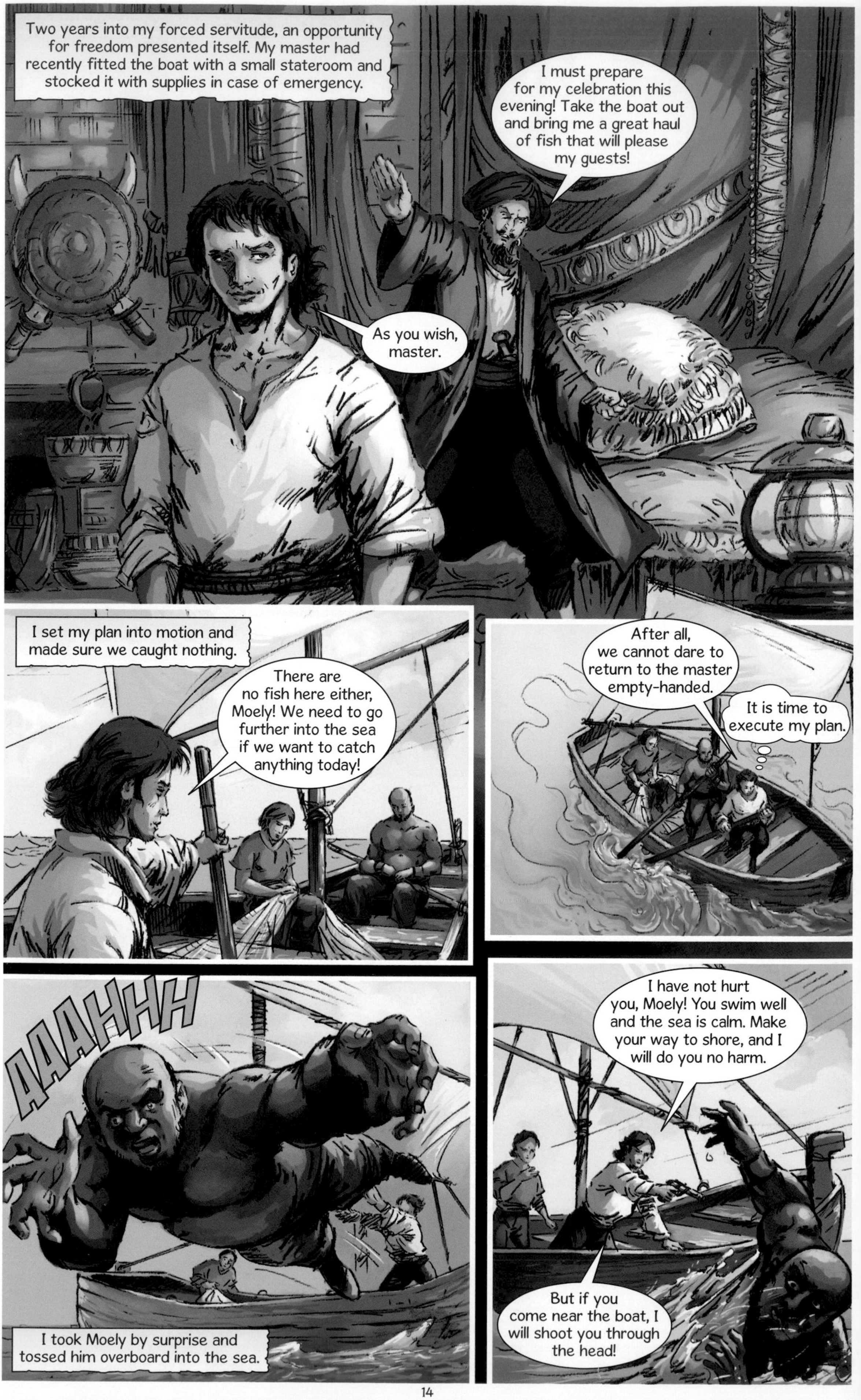
Two years into my forced servitude, an opportunity for freedom presented itself. My master had recently fitted the boat with a small stateroom and stocked it with supplies in case of emergency.
I must prepare for my celebration this evening! Take the boat out and bring me a great haul of fish that will please my guests!
As you wish, master.
I set my plan into motion and made sure we caught nothing.
There are no fish here either, Moely! We need to go further into the sea if we want to catch anything today!
After all, we cannot dare to return to the master empty-handed.
It is time to execute my plan.
AAAHHH
I took Moely by surprise and tossed him overboard into the sea.
I have not hurt you, Moely! You swim well and the sea is calm. Make your way to shore, and I will do you no harm.
But if you come near the boat, I will shoot you through the head!

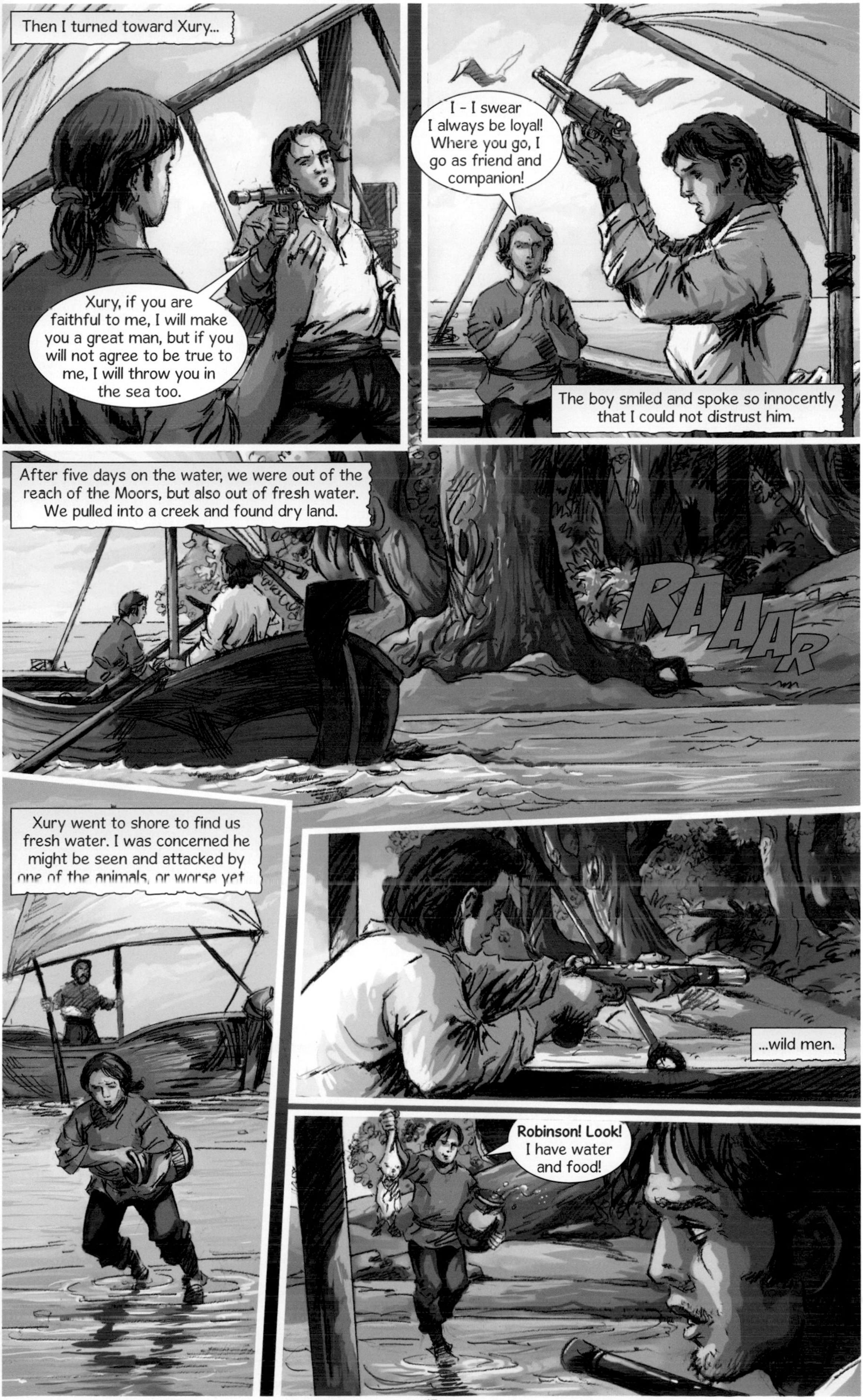

Then I turned toward Xury...
Xury, if you are faithful to me, I will make you a great man, but if you will not agree to be true to me, I will throw you in the sea too.
I - I swear I always be loyal! Where you go, I go as friend and companion!
The boy smiled and spoke so innocently that I could not distrust him.
After five days on the water, we were out of the reach of the Moors, but also out of fresh water. We pulled into a creek and found dry land.
RAAAAR
Xury went to shore to find us fresh water. I was concerned he might be seen and attacked by one of the animals, or worse yet
...wild men.
Robinson! Look! I have water and food!

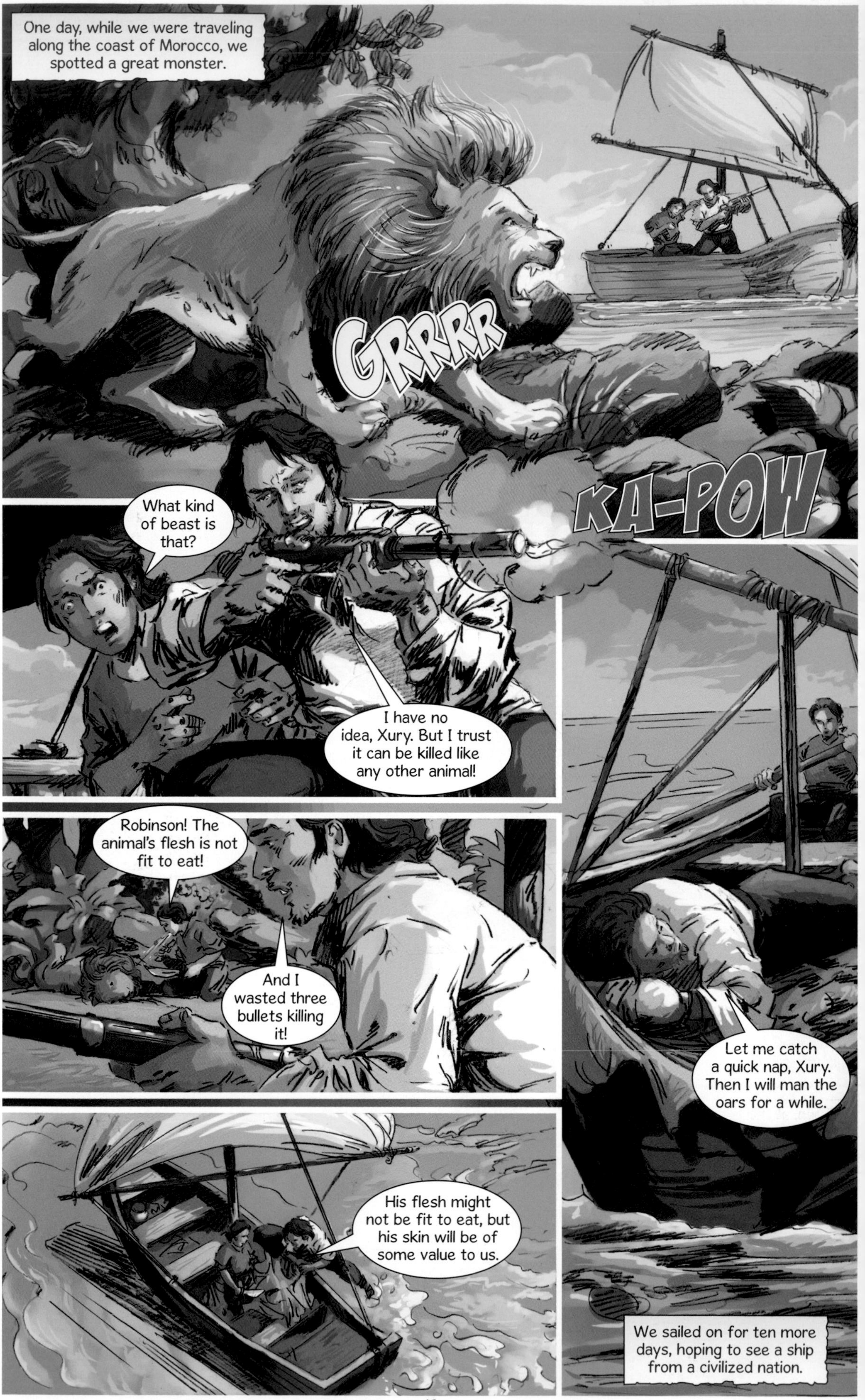
One day, while we were traveling along the coast of Morocco, we spotted a great monster.
GRRRR
KA-POW
What kind of beast is that?
I have no idea, Xury. But I trust it can be killed like any other animal!
Robinson! The animal's flesh is not fit to eat!
And I wasted three bullets killing it!
His flesh might not be fit to eat, but his skin will be of some value to us.
Let me catch a quick nap, Xury. Then I will man the oars for a while.
We sailed on for ten more days, hoping to see a ship from a civilized nation.

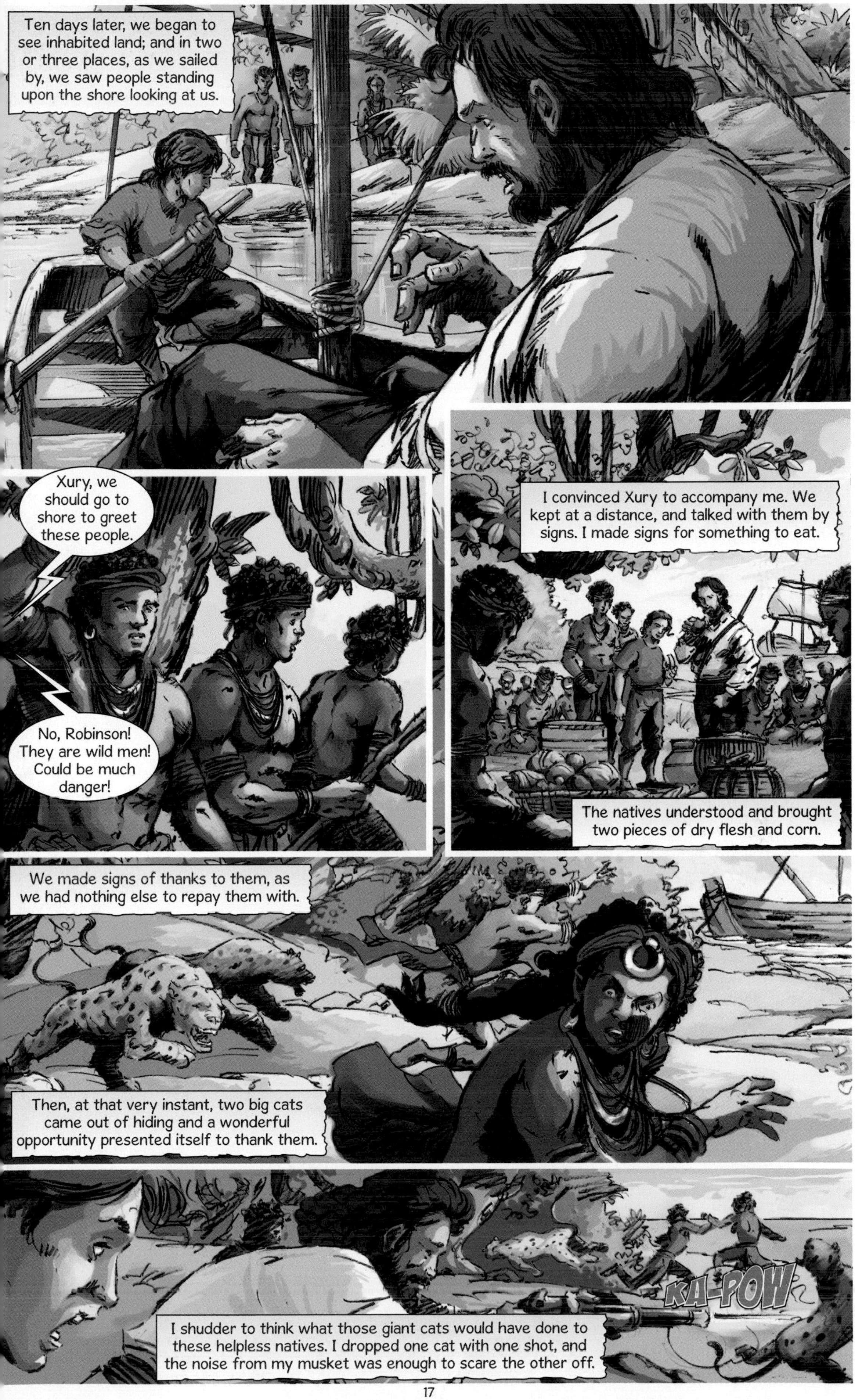
Ten days later, we began to see inhabited land; and in two or three places, as we sailed by, we saw people standing upon the shore looking at us.
Xury, we should go to shore to greet these people.
No, Robinson! They are wild men! Could be much danger!
I convinced Xury to accompany me. We kept at a distance, and talked with them by signs. I made signs for something to eat.
The natives understood and brought two pieces of dry flesh and corn.
We made signs of thanks to them, as we had nothing else to repay them with.
Then, at that very instant, two big cats came out of hiding and a wonderful opportunity presented itself to thank them.
KA-POW
I shudder to think what those giant cats would have done to these helpless natives. I dropped one cat with one shot, and the noise from my musket was enough to scare the other off.

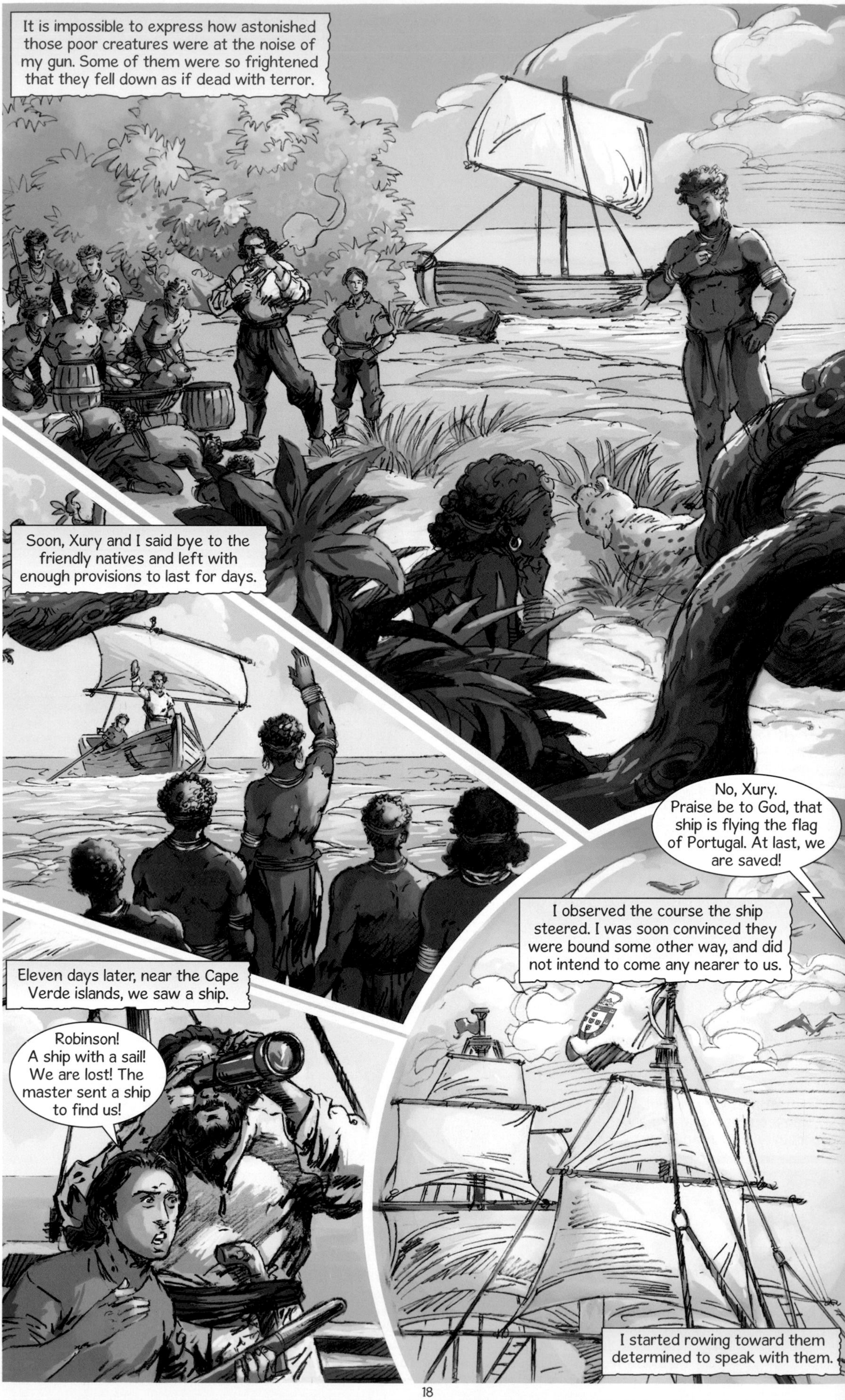

It is impossible to express how astonished those poor creatures were at the noise of my gun. Some of them were so frightened that they fell down as if dead with terror.
Soon, Xury and I said bye to the friendly natives and left with enough provisions to last for days.
Eleven days later, near the Cape Verde islands, we saw a ship.
Robinson! A ship with a sail! We are lost! The master sent a ship to find us!
No, Xury. Praise be to God, that ship is flying the flag of Portugal. At last, we are saved!
I observed the course the ship steered. I was soon convinced they were bound some other way, and did not intend to come any nearer to us.
I started rowing toward them determined to speak with them.

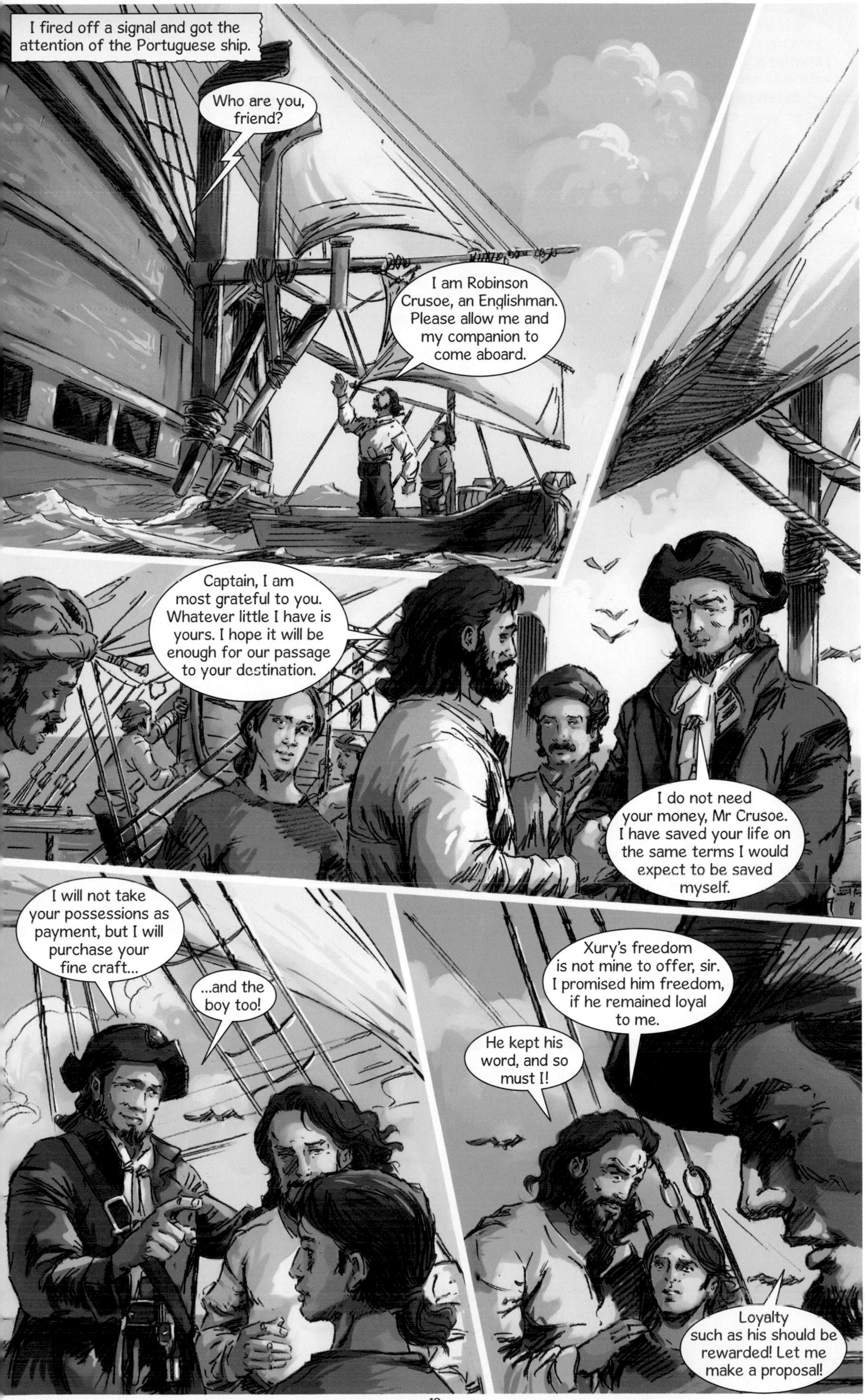
I fired off a signal and got the attention of the Portuguese ship.
Who are you, friend?
I am Robinson Crusoe, an Englishman. Please allow me and my companion to come aboard.
Captain, I am most grateful to you. Whatever little I have is yours. I hope it will be enough for our passage to your destination.
I do not need your money, Mr Crusoe. I have saved your life on the same terms I would expect to be saved myself.
I will not take your possessions as payment, but I will purchase your fine craft...
...and the boy too!
Xury's freedom is not mine to offer, sir. I promised him freedom, if he remained loyal to me.
He kept his word, and so must I!
Loyalty such as his should be rewarded! Let me make a proposal!

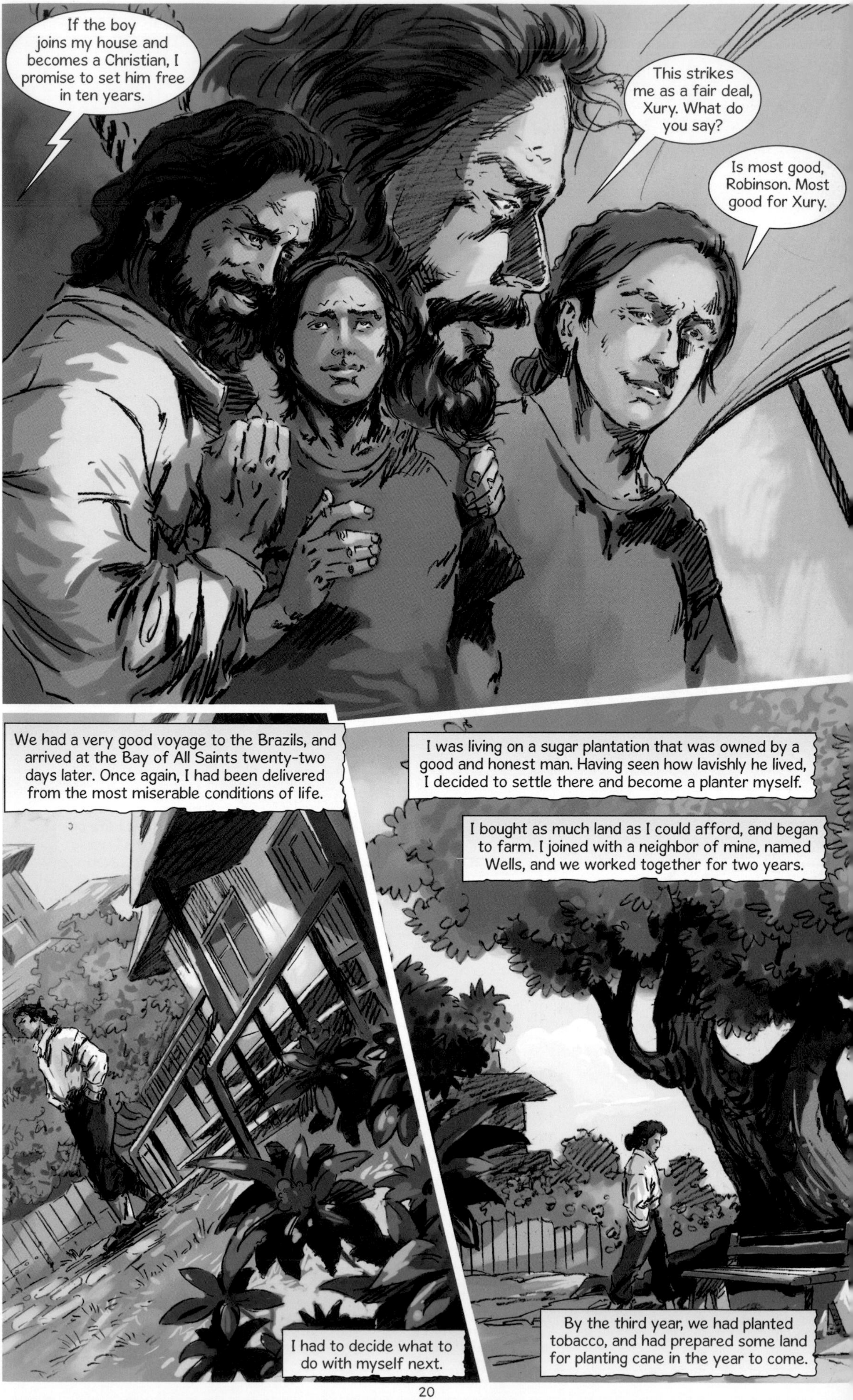
If the boy joins my house and becomes a Christian, I promise to set him free in ten years.
This strikes me as a fair deal, Xury. What do you say?
Is most good, Robinson. Most good for Xury.
We had a very good voyage to the Brazils, and arrived at the Bay of All Saints twenty-two days later. Once again, I had been delivered from the most miserable conditions of life.
I had to decide what to do with myself next.
I was living on a sugar plantation that was owned by a good and honest man. Having seen how lavishly he lived, I decided to settle there and become a planter myself.
I bought as much land as I could afford, and began to farm. I joined with a neighbor of mine, named Wells, and we worked together for two years.
By the third year, we had planted tobacco, and had prepared some land for planting cane in the year to come.

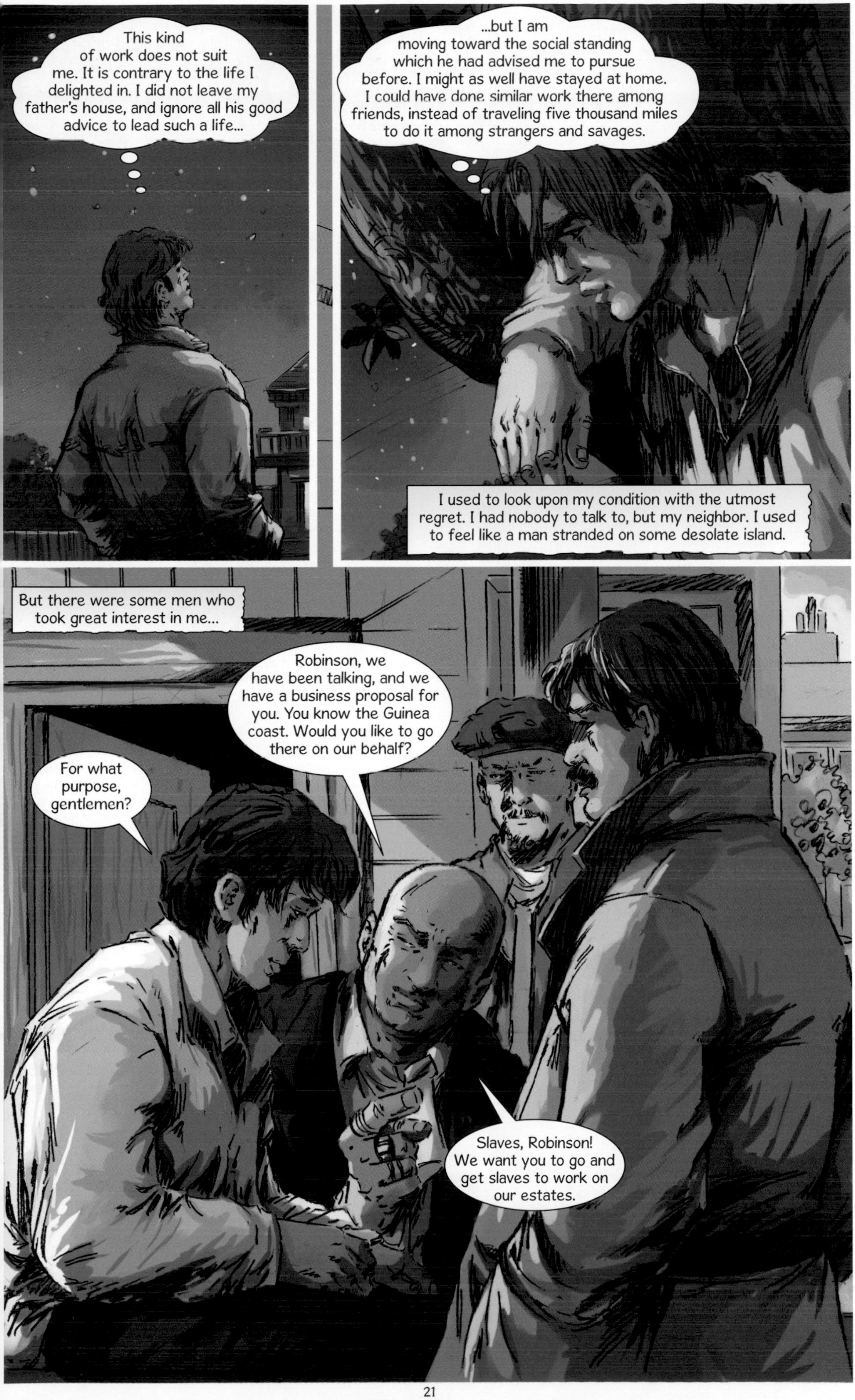
This kind of work does not suit me. It is contrary to the life I delighted in. I did not leave my father's house, and ignore all his good advice to lead such a life...
...but I am moving toward the social standing which he had advised me to pursue before. I might as well have stayed at home. I could have done similar work there among friends, instead of traveling five thousand miles to do it among strangers and savages.
I used to look upon my condition with the utmost regret. I had nobody to talk to, but my neighbor. I used to feel like a man stranded on some desolate island.
But there were some men who took great interest in me...
Robinson, we have been talking, and we have a business proposal for you. You know the Guinea coast. Would you like to go there on our behalf?
For what purpose, gentlemen?
Slaves, Robinson! We want you to go and get slaves to work on our estates.

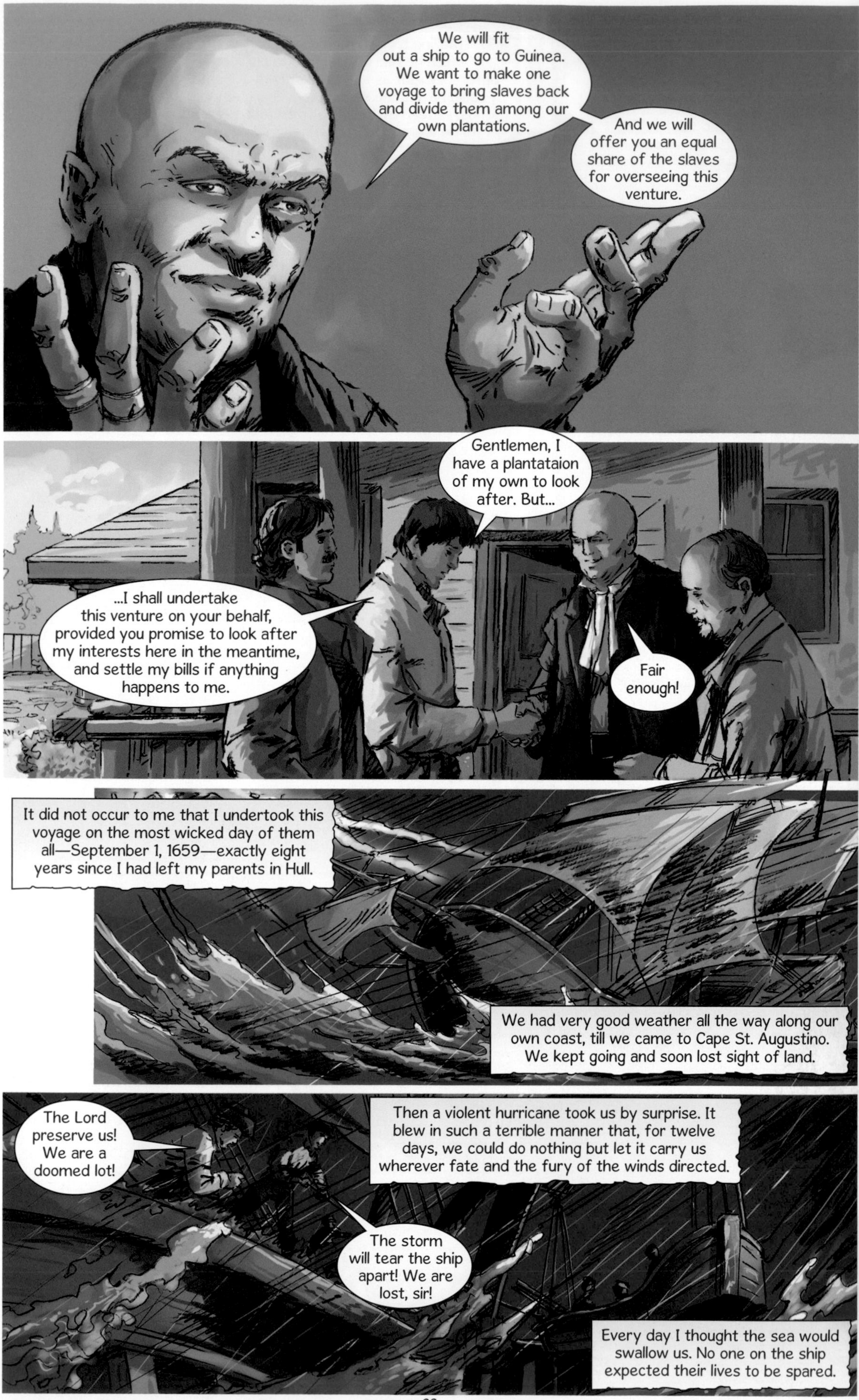
We will fit out a ship to go to Guinea. We want to make one voyage to bring slaves back and divide them among our own plantations.
And we will offer you an equal share of the slaves for overseeing this venture.
Gentlemen, I have a plantataion of my own to look after. But...
...I shall undertake this venture on your behalf, provided you promise to look after my interests here in the meantime, and settle my bills if anything happens to me.
Fair enough!
It did not occur to me that I undertook this voyage on the most wicked day of them all—September 1, 1659—exactly eight years since I had left my parents in Hull.
We had very good weather all the way along our own coast, till we came to Cape St. Augustino. We kept going and soon lost sight of land.
The Lord preserve us! We are a doomed lot!
Then a violent hurricane took us by surprise. It blew in such a terrible manner that, for twelve days, we could do nothing but let it carry us wherever fate and the fury of the winds directed.
The storm will tear the ship apart! We are lost, sir!
Every day I thought the sea would swallow us. No one on the ship expected their lives to be spared.

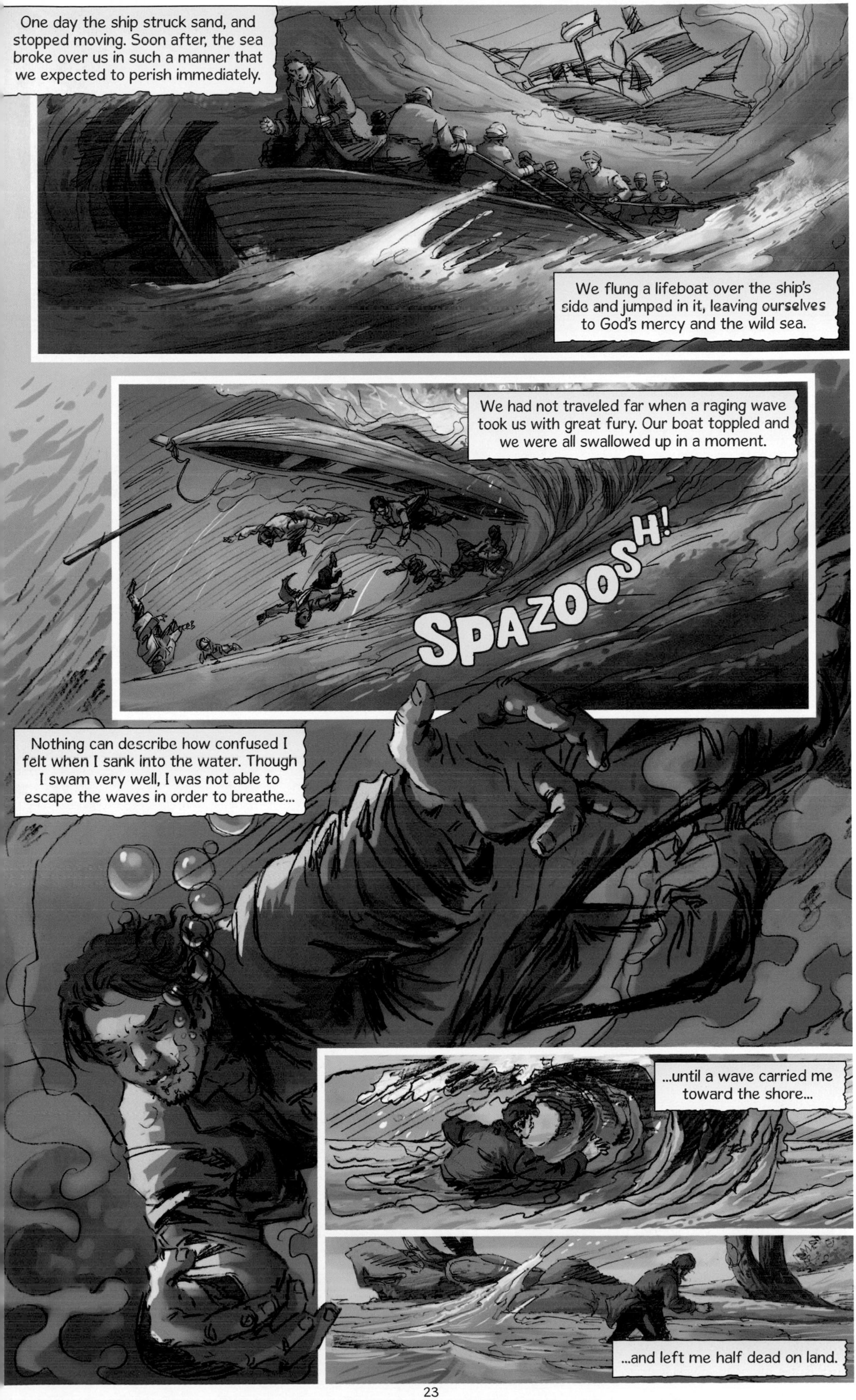
One day the ship struck sand, and stopped moving. Soon after, the sea broke over us in such a manner that we expected to perish immediately.
We flung a lifeboat over the ship's side and jumped in it, leaving ourselves to God's mercy and the wild sea.
We had not traveled far when a raging wave took us with great fury. Our boat toppled and we were all swallowed up in a moment.
SPAZOOSH!
Nothing can describe how confused I felt when I sank into the water. Though I swam very well, I was not able to escape the waves in order to breathe...
...until a wave carried me toward the shore...
...and left me half dead on land.

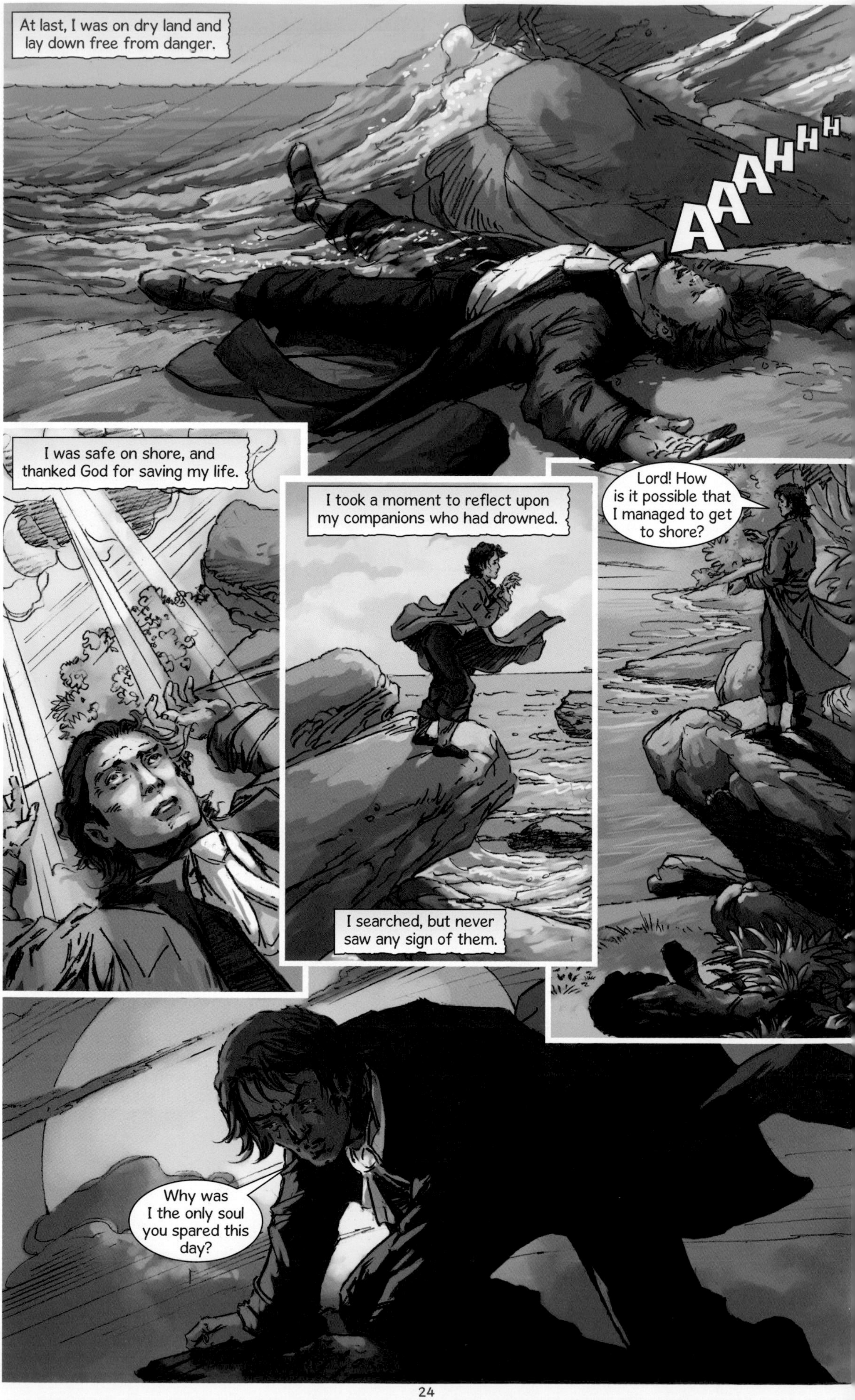
At last, I was on dry land and lay down free from danger.
AAAHHH
I was safe on shore, and thanked God for saving my life.
I took a moment to reflect upon my companions who had drowned.
I searched, but never saw any sign of them.
Lord! How is it possible that I managed to get to shore?
Why was I the only soul you spared this day?

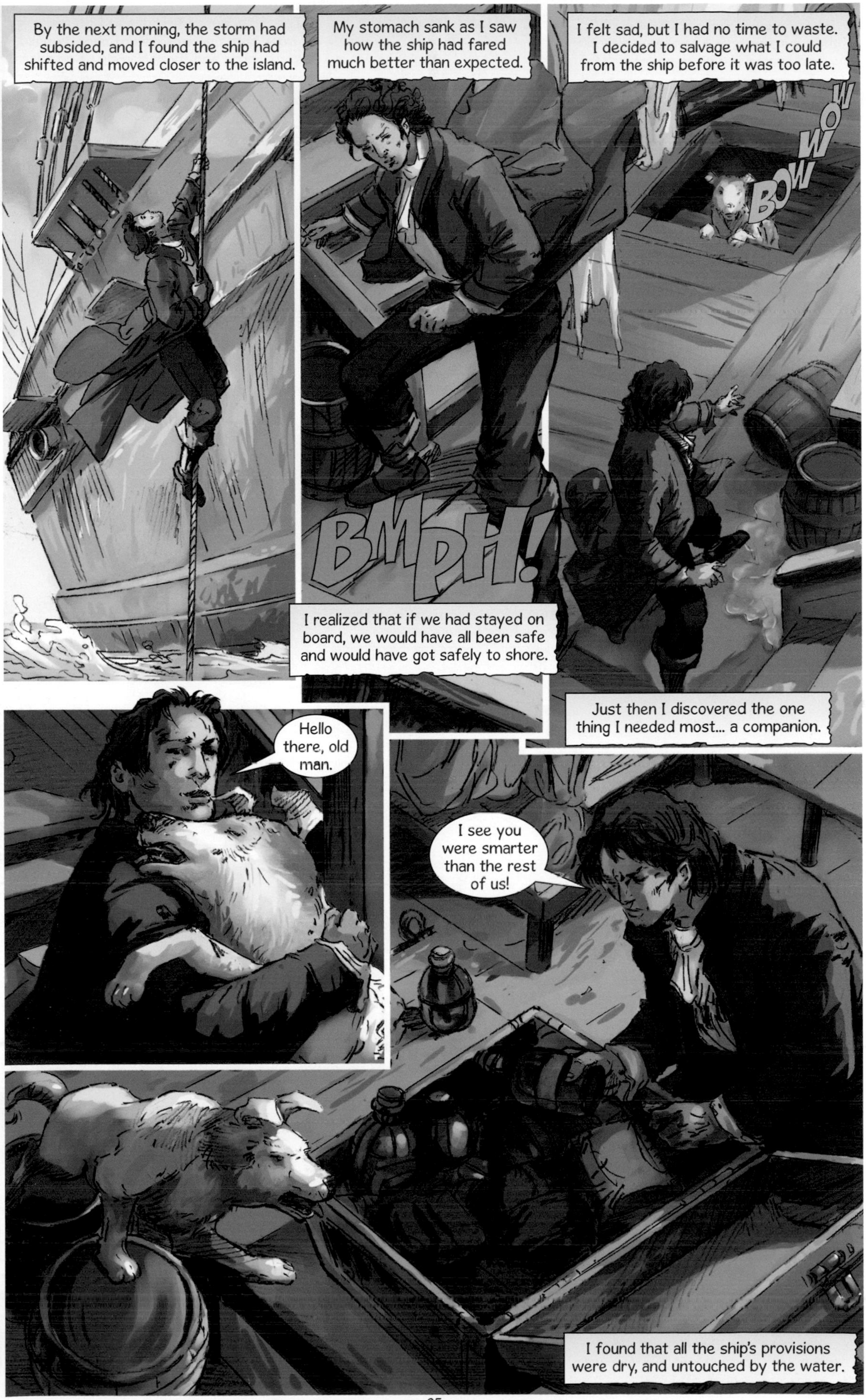
By the next morning, the storm had subsided, and I found the ship had shifted and moved closer to the island.
My stomach sank as I saw how the ship had fared much better than expected.
BMPH!
I realized that if we had stayed on board, we would have all been safe and would have got safely to shore.
I felt sad, but I had no time to waste. I decided to salvage what I could from the ship before it was too late.
BOW WOW
Just then I discovered the one thing I needed most... a companion.
Hello there, old man.
I see you were smarter than the rest of us!
I found that all the ship's provisions were dry, and untouched by the water.

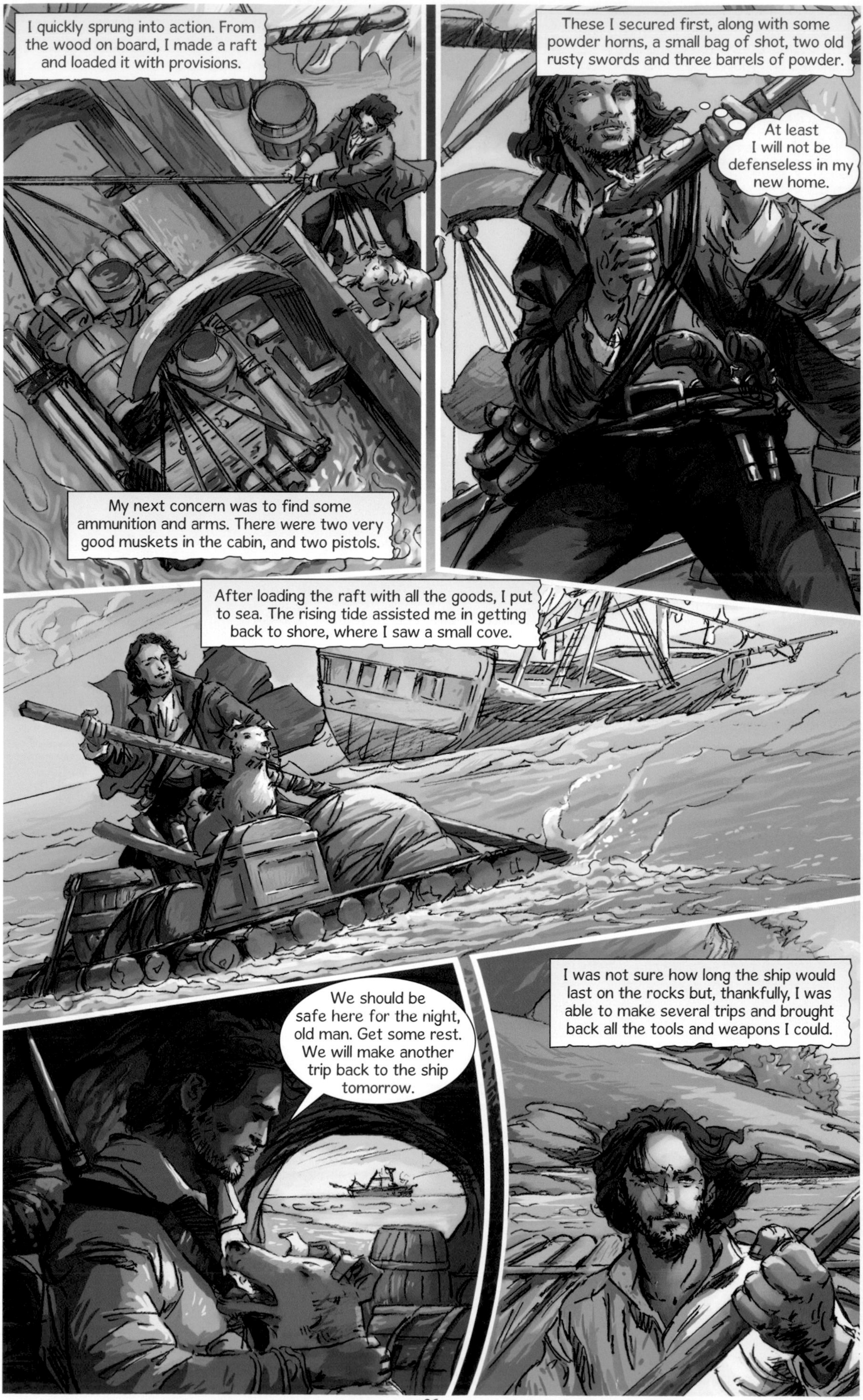
I quickly sprung into action. From the wood on board, I made a raft and loaded it with provisions.
My next concern was to find some ammunition and arms. There were two very good muskets in the cabin, and two pistols.
These I secured first, along with some powder horns, a small bag of shot, two old rusty swords and three barrels of powder.
At least I will not be defenseless in my new home.
After loading the raft with all the goods, I put to sea. The rising tide assisted me in getting back to shore, where I saw a small cove.
We should be safe here for the night, old man. Get some rest. We will make another trip back to the ship tomorrow.
I was not sure how long the ship would last on the rocks but, thankfully, I was able to make several trips and brought back all the tools and weapons I could.

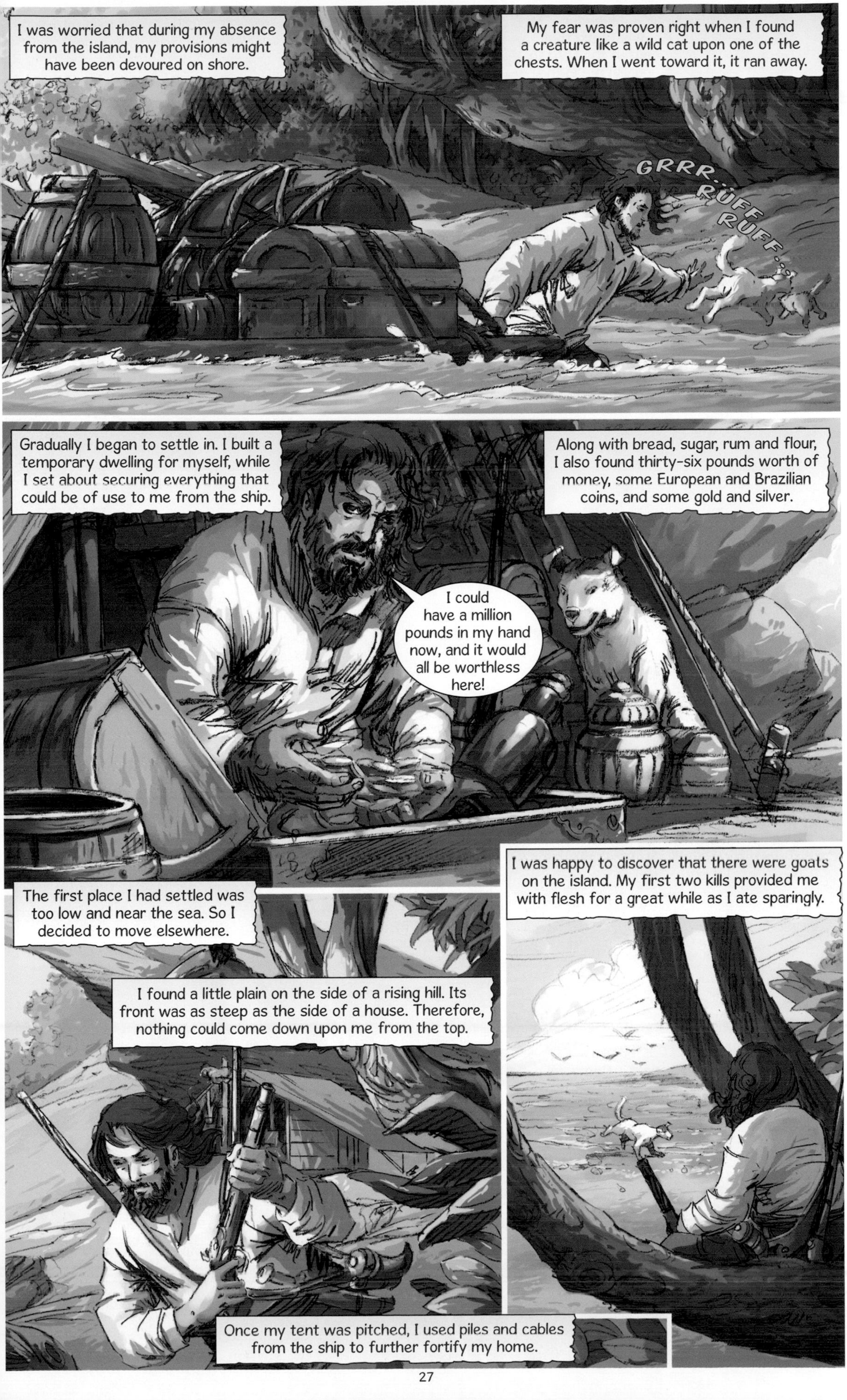
I was worried that during my absence from the island, my provisions might have been devoured on shore.
My fear was proven right when I found a creature like a wild cat upon one of the chests. When I went toward it, it ran away.
GRRR...
RUFF RUFF...
Gradually I began to settle in. I built a temporary dwelling for myself, while I set about securing everything that could be of use to me from the ship.
Along with bread, sugar, rum and flour, I also found thirty-six pounds worth of money, some European and Brazilian coins, and some gold and silver.
I could have a million pounds in my hand now, and it would all be worthless here!
The first place I had settled was too low and near the sea. So I decided to move elsewhere.
I found a little plain on the side of a rising hill. Its front was as steep as the side of a house. Therefore, nothing could come down upon me from the top.
I was happy to discover that there were goats on the island. My first two kills provided me with flesh for a great while as I ate sparingly.
Once my tent was pitched, I used piles and cables from the ship to further fortify my home.

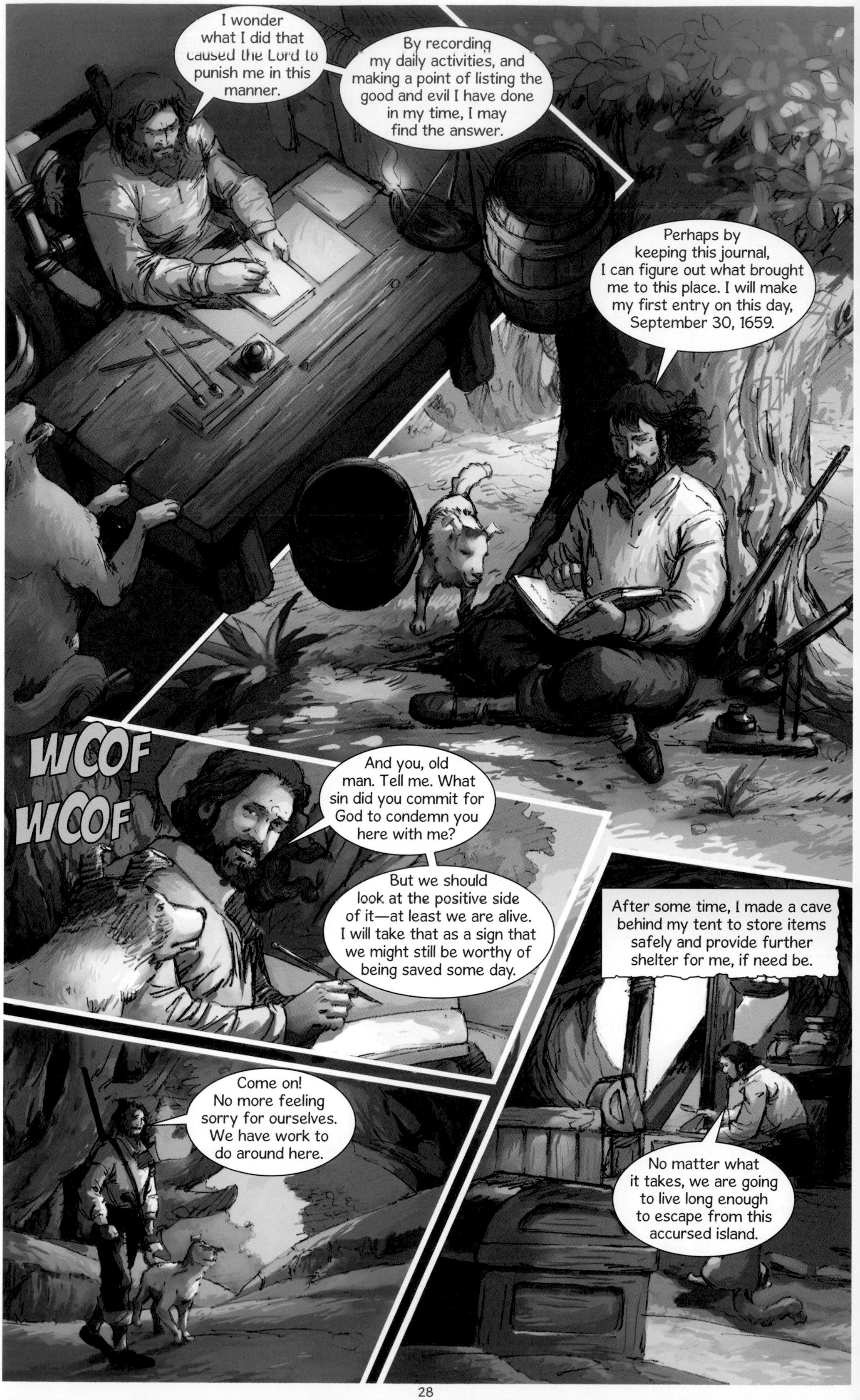
I wonder what I did that caused the Lord to punish me in this manner.
By recording my daily activities, and making a point of listing the good and evil I have done in my time, I may find the answer.
Perhaps by keeping this journal, I can figure out what brought me to this place. I will make my first entry on this day, September 30, 1659.
WOOF WOOF
And you, old man. Tell me. What sin did you commit for God to condemn you here with me?
But we should look at the positive side of it—at least we are alive. I will take that as a sign that we might still be worthy of being saved some day.
Come on! No more feeling sorry for ourselves. We have work to do around here.
After some time, I made a cave behind my tent to store items safely and provide further shelter for me, if need be.
No matter what it takes, we are going to live long enough to escape from this accursed island.

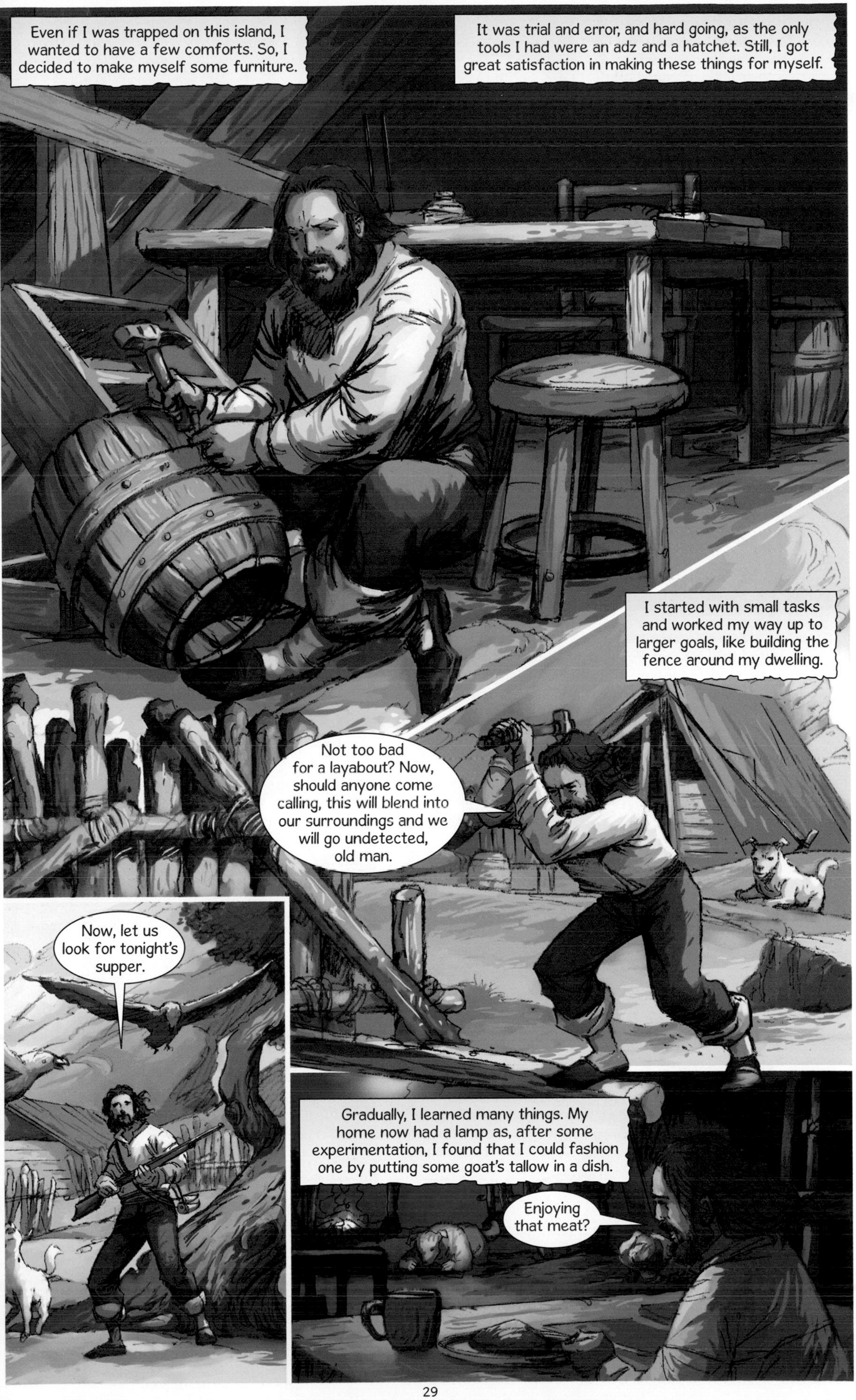
Even if I was trapped on this island, I wanted to have a few comforts. So, I decided to make myself some furniture.
It was trial and error, and hard going, as the only tools I had were an adz and a hatchet. Still, I got great satisfaction in making these things for myself.
I started with small tasks and worked my way up to larger goals, like building the fence around my dwelling.
Not too bad for a layabout? Now, should anyone come calling, this will blend into our surroundings and we will go undetected, old man.
Now, let us look for tonight's supper.
Gradually, I learned many things. My home now had a lamp as, after some experimentation, I found that I could fashion one by putting some goat's tallow in a dish.
Enjoying that meat?

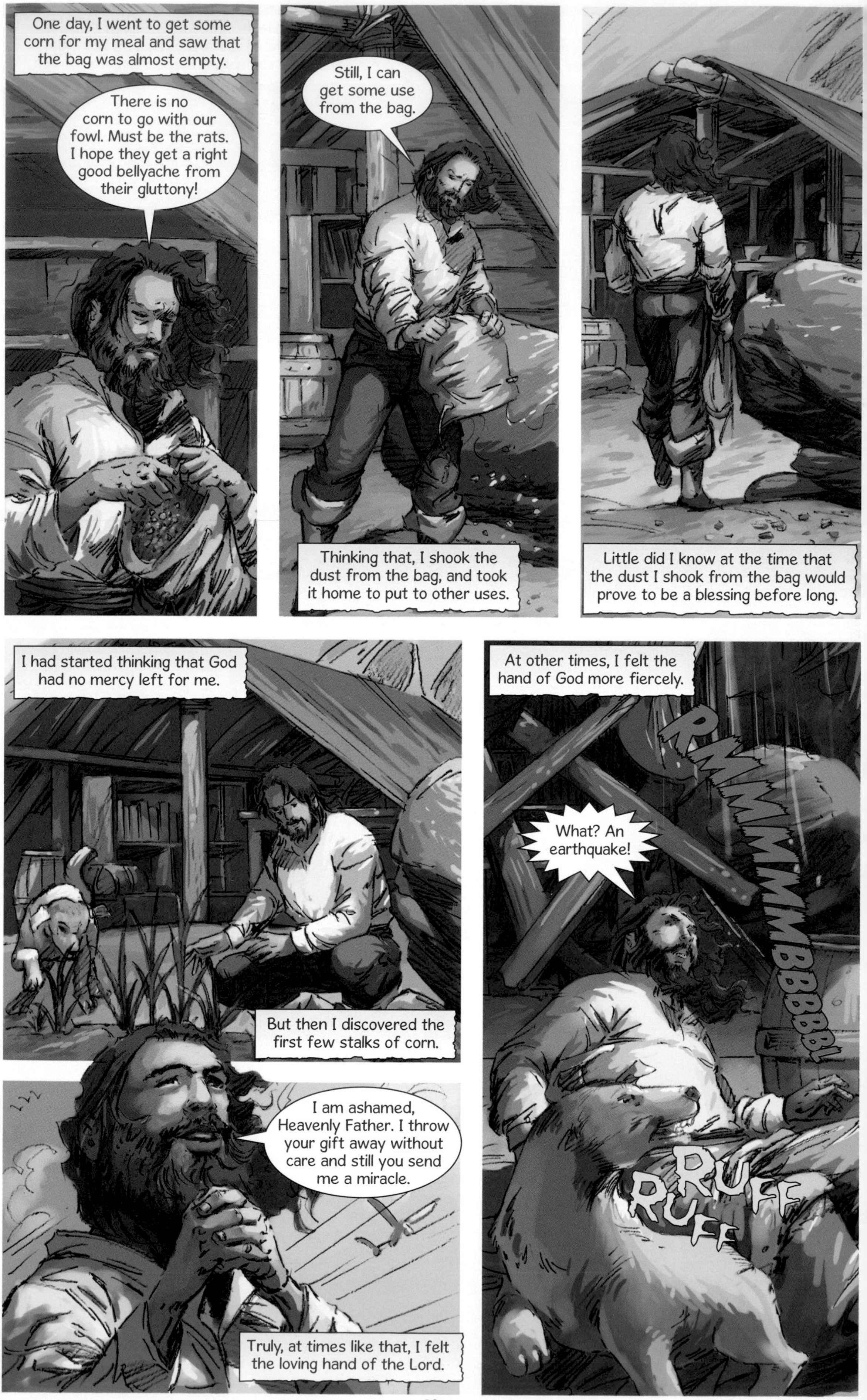
One day, I went to get some corn for my meal and saw that the bag was almost empty.
There is no corn to go with our fowl. Must be the rats. I hope they get a right good bellyache from their gluttony!
Still, I can get some use from the bag.
Thinking that, I shook the dust from the bag, and took it home to put to other uses.
Little did I know at the time that the dust I shook from the bag would prove to be a blessing before long.
I had started thinking that God had no mercy left for me.
But then I discovered the first few stalks of corn.
I am ashamed, Heavenly Father. I throw your gift away without care and still you send me a miracle.
Truly, at times like that, I felt the loving hand of the Lord.
At other times, I felt the hand of God more fiercely.
RMMMMMMMBBBBBL
What? An earthquake!
RUFF
RUFF

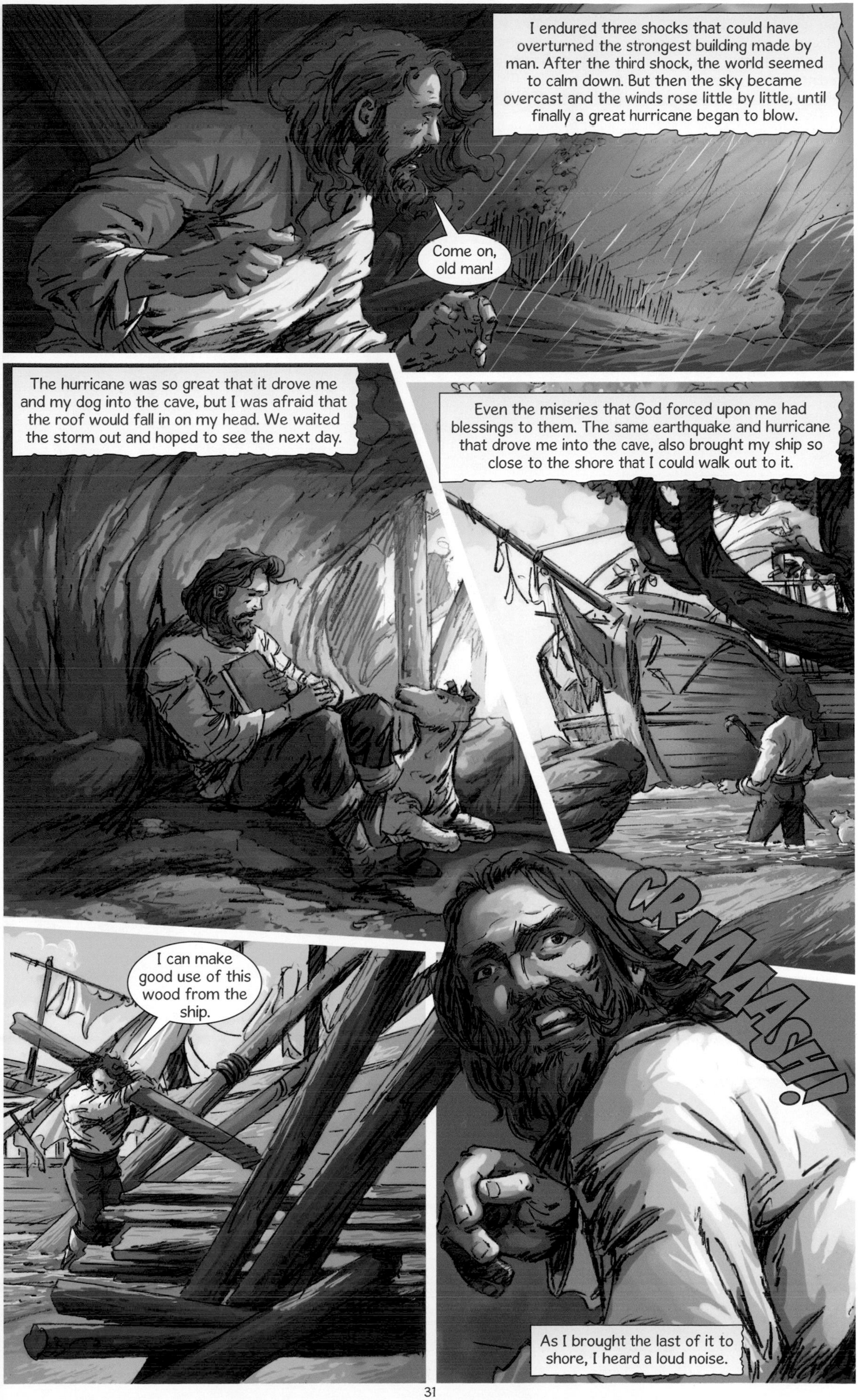
I endured three shocks that could have overturned the strongest building made by man. After the third shock, the world seemed to calm down. But then the sky became overcast and the winds rose little by little, until finally a great hurricane began to blow.
Come on, old man!
The hurricane was so great that it drove me and my dog into the cave, but I was afraid that the roof would fall in on my head. We waited the storm out and hoped to see the next day.
Even the miseries that God forced upon me had blessings to them. The same earthquake and hurricane that drove me into the cave, also brought my ship so close to the shore that I could walk out to it.
I can make good use of this wood from the ship.
As I brought the last of it to shore, I heard a loud noise.
CRAAAASH!!

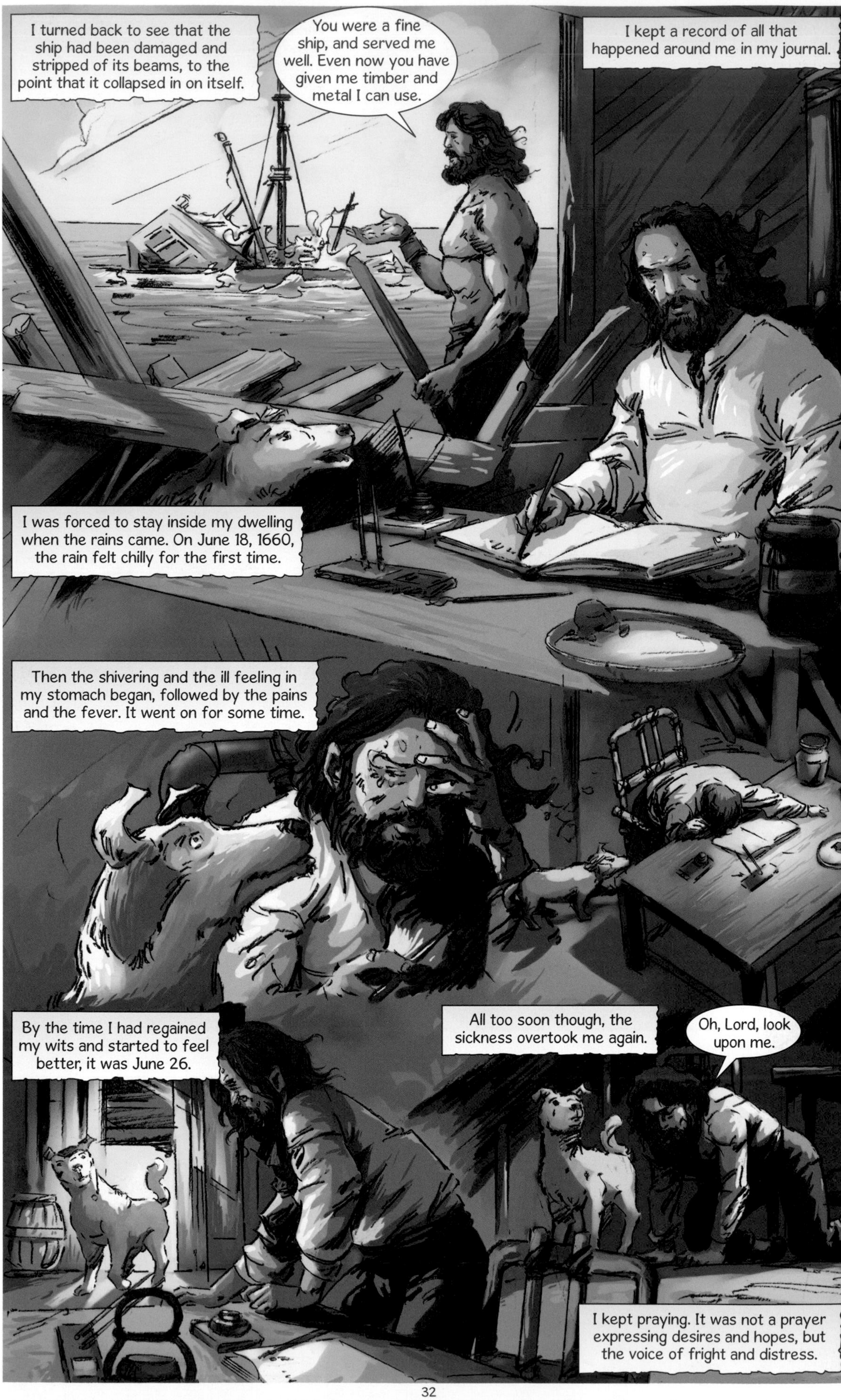

I turned back to see that the ship had been damaged and stripped of its beams, to the point that it collapsed in on itself.
You were a fine ship, and served me well. Even now you have given me timber and metal I can use.
I kept a record of all that happened around me in my journal.
I was forced to stay inside my dwelling when the rains came. On June 18, 1660, the rain felt chilly for the first time.
Then the shivering and the ill feeling in my stomach began, followed by the pains and the fever. It went on for some time.
By the time I had regained my wits and started to feel better, it was June 26.
All too soon though, the sickness overtook me again.
Oh, Lord, look upon me.
I kept praying. It was not a prayer expressing desires and hopes, but the voice of fright and distress.

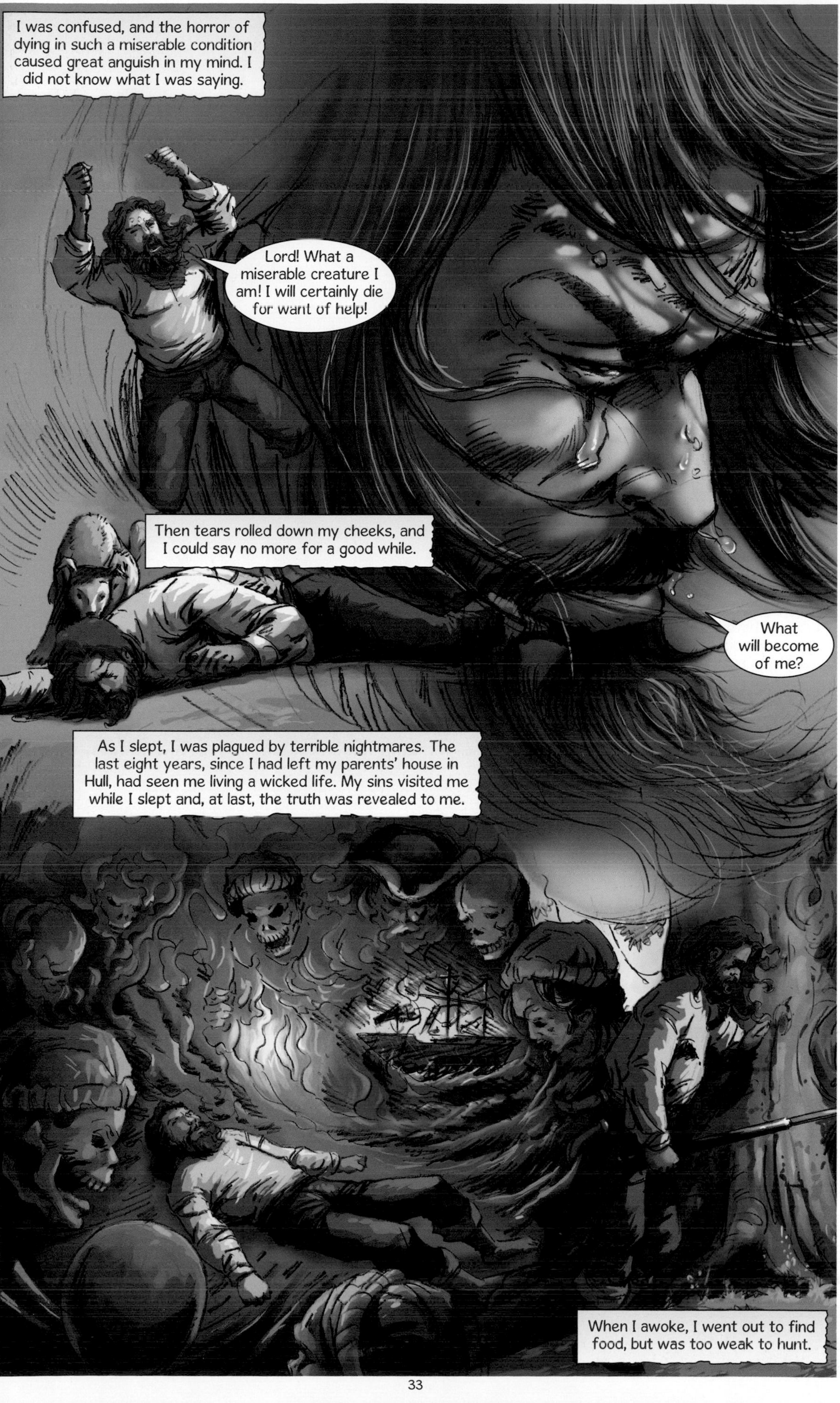
I was confused, and the horror of dying in such a miserable condition caused great anguish in my mind. I did not know what I was saying.
Lord! What a miserable creature I am! I will certainly die for want of help!
Then tears rolled down my cheeks, and I could say no more for a good while.
What will become of me?
As I slept, I was plagued by terrible nightmares. The last eight years, since I had left my parents' house in Hull, had seen me living a wicked life. My sins visited me while I slept and, at last, the truth was revealed to me.
When I awoke, I went out to find food, but was too weak to hunt.

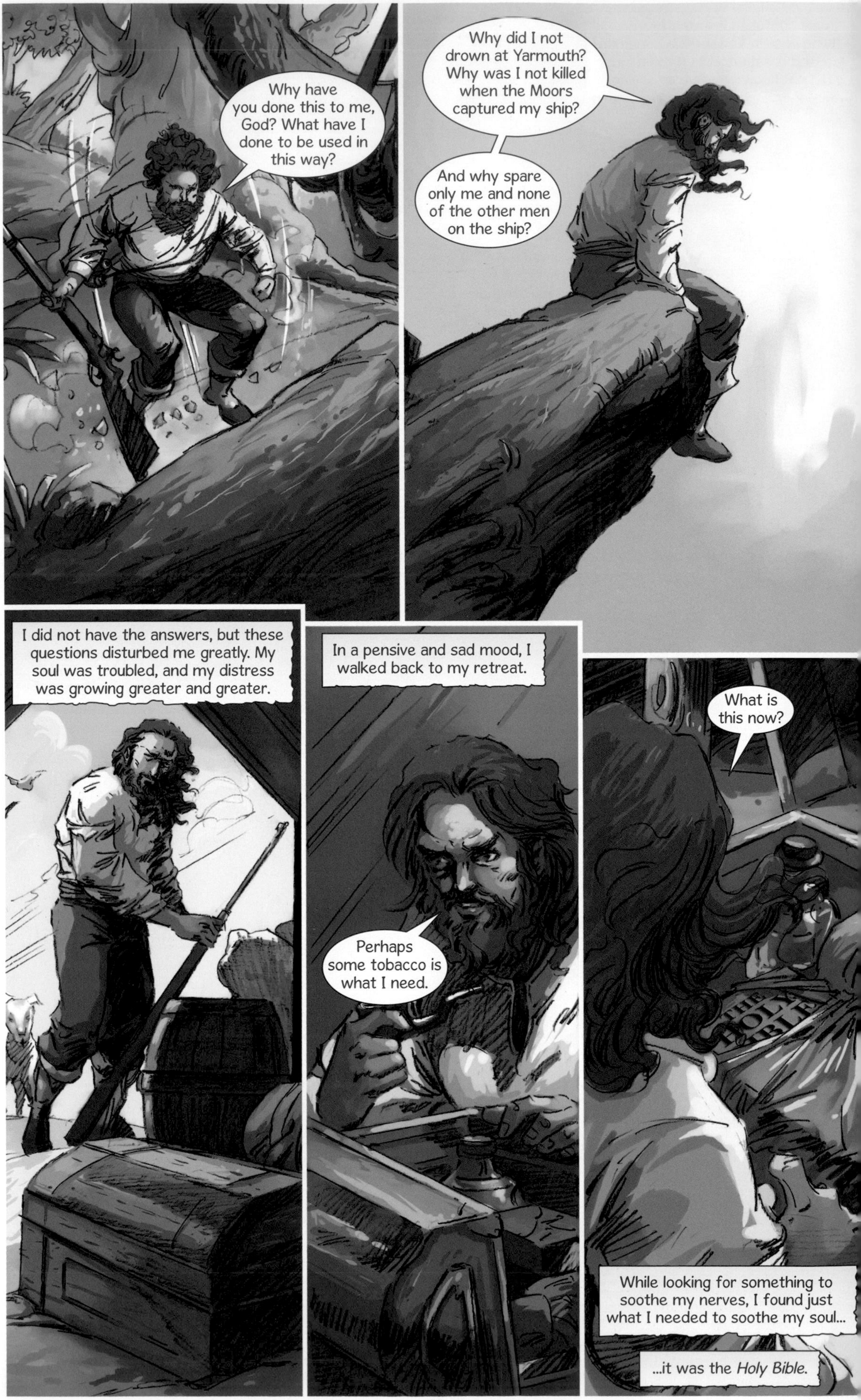
Why have you done this to me, God? What have I done to be used in this way?
Why did I not drown at Yarmouth? Why was I not killed when the Moors captured my ship?
And why spare only me and none of the other men on the ship?
I did not have the answers, but these questions disturbed me greatly. My soul was troubled, and my distress was growing greater and greater.
In a pensive and sad mood, I walked back to my retreat.
Perhaps some tobacco is what I need.
What is this now?
THE HOLY BIBLE
While looking for something to soothe my nerves, I found just what I needed to soothe my soul...
...it was the *Holy Bible*.

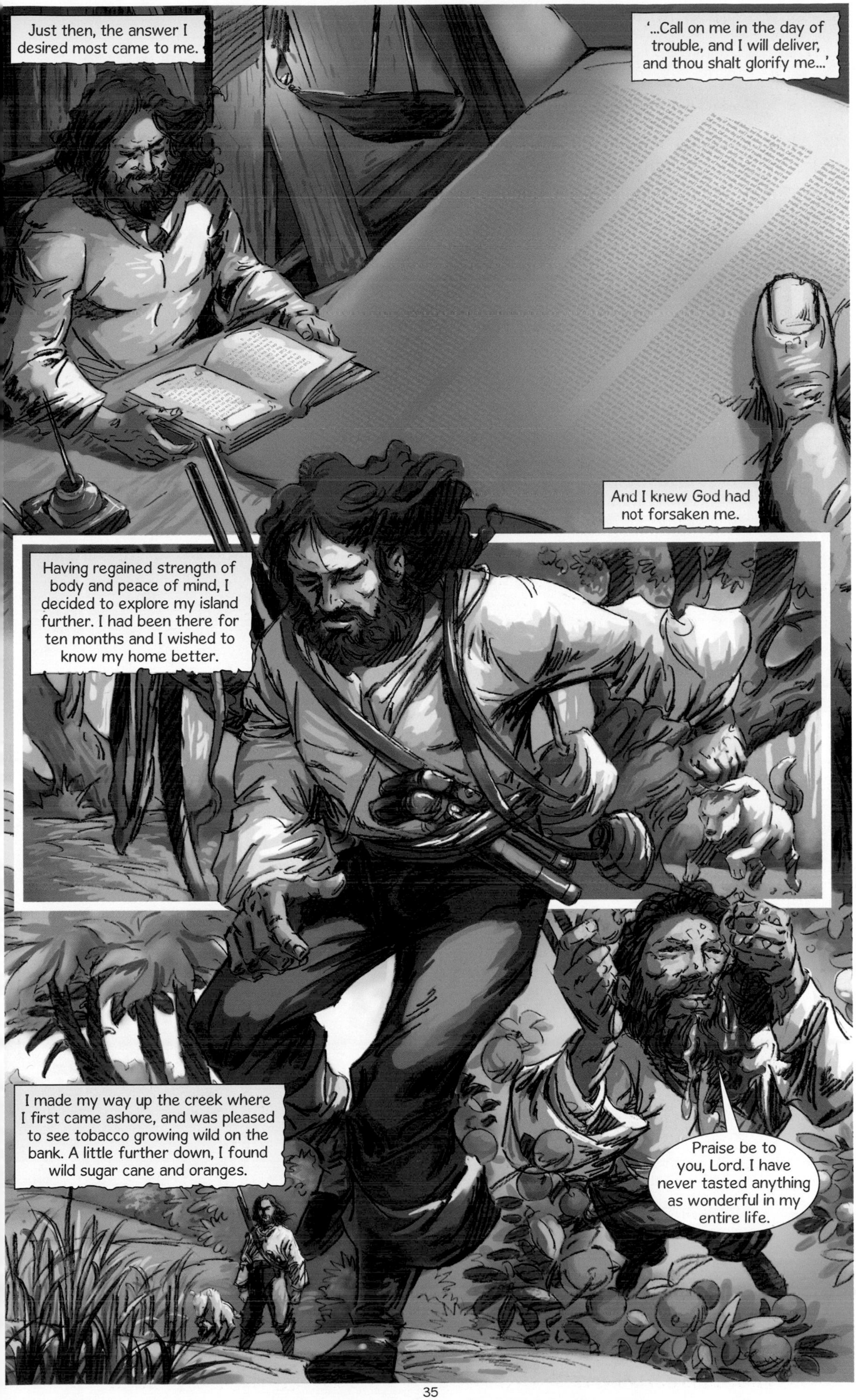
Just then, the answer I desired most came to me.
'...Call on me in the day of trouble, and I will deliver, and thou shalt glorify me...'
And I knew God had not forsaken me.
Having regained strength of body and peace of mind, I decided to explore my island further. I had been there for ten months and I wished to know my home better.
I made my way up the creek where I first came ashore, and was pleased to see tobacco growing wild on the bank. A little further down, I found wild sugar cane and oranges.
Praise be to you, Lord. I have never tasted anything as wonderful in my entire life.

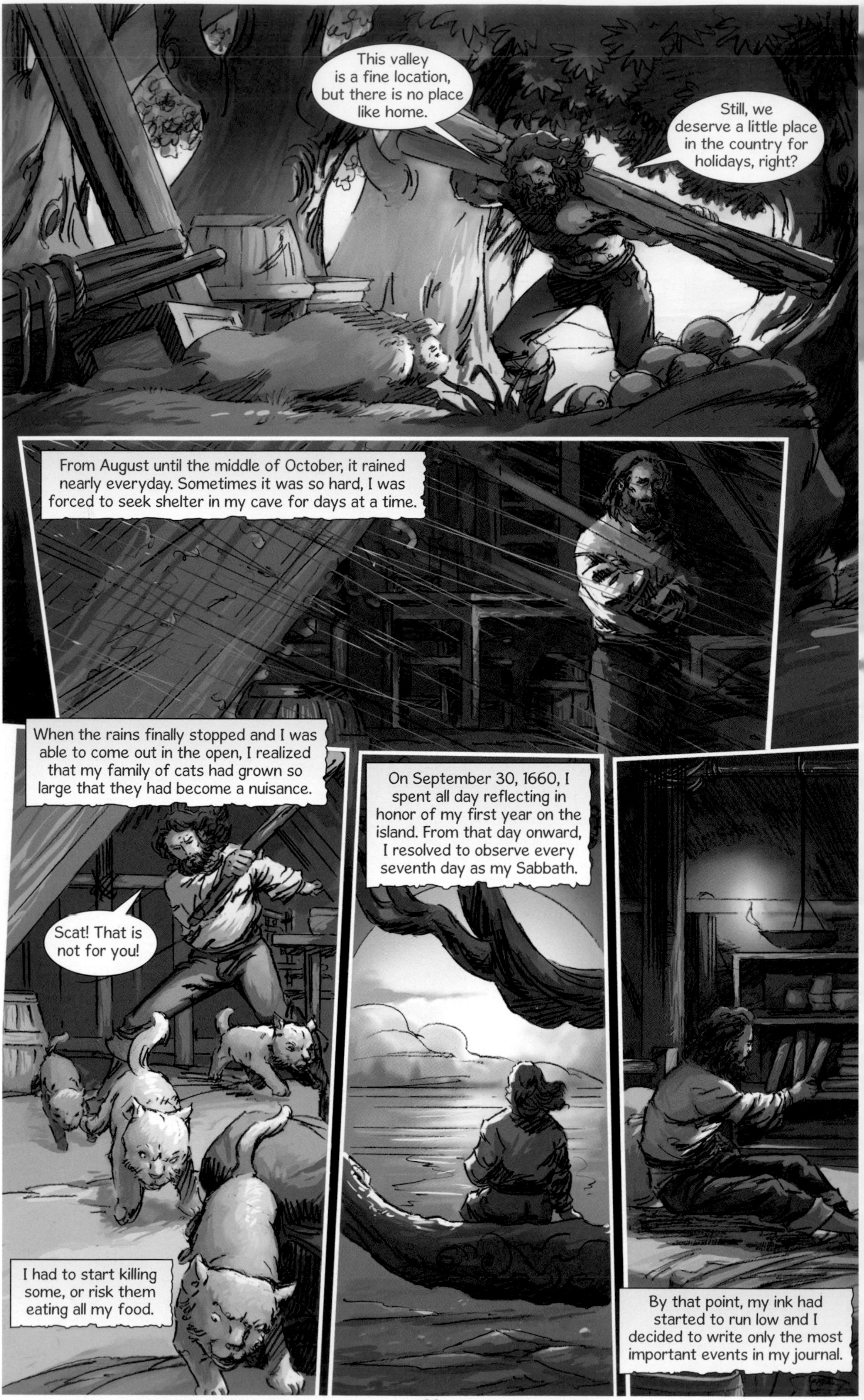

This valley is a fine location, but there is no place like home.
Still, we deserve a little place in the country for holidays, right?
From August until the middle of October, it rained nearly everyday. Sometimes it was so hard, I was forced to seek shelter in my cave for days at a time.
When the rains finally stopped and I was able to come out in the open, I realized that my family of cats had grown so large that they had become a nuisance.
Scat! That is not for you!
I had to start killing some, or risk them eating all my food.
On September 30, 1660, I spent all day reflecting in honor of my first year on the island. From that day onward, I resolved to observe every seventh day as my Sabbath.
By that point, my ink had started to run low and I decided to write only the most important events in my journal.

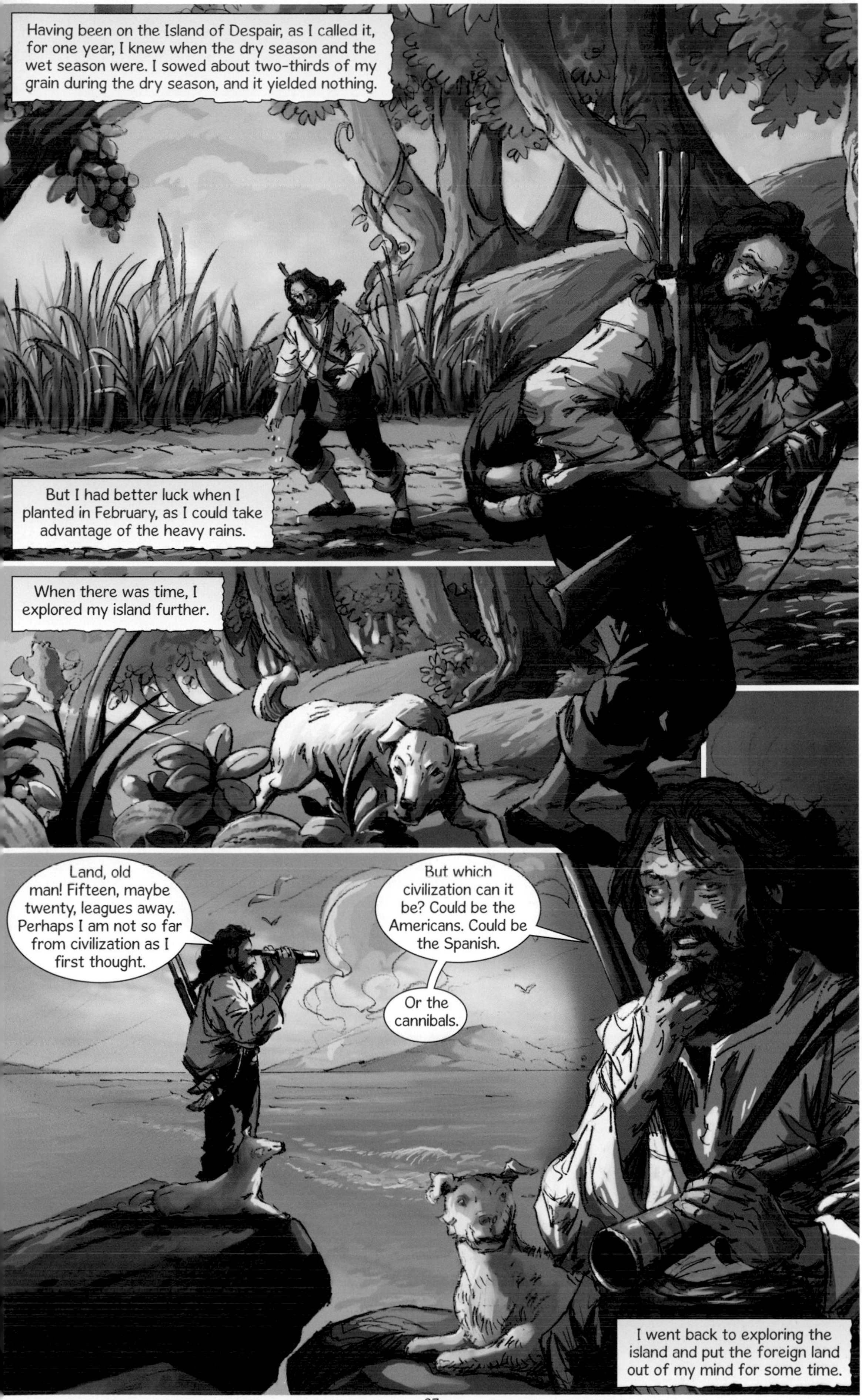
Having been on the Island of Despair, as I called it, for one year, I knew when the dry season and the wet season were. I sowed about two-thirds of my grain during the dry season, and it yielded nothing.
But I had better luck when I planted in February, as I could take advantage of the heavy rains.
When there was time, I explored my island further.
Land, old man! Fifteen, maybe twenty, leagues away. Perhaps I am not so far from civilization as I first thought.
But which civilization can it be? Could be the Americans. Could be the Spanish.
Or the cannibals.
I went back to exploring the island and put the foreign land out of my mind for some time.

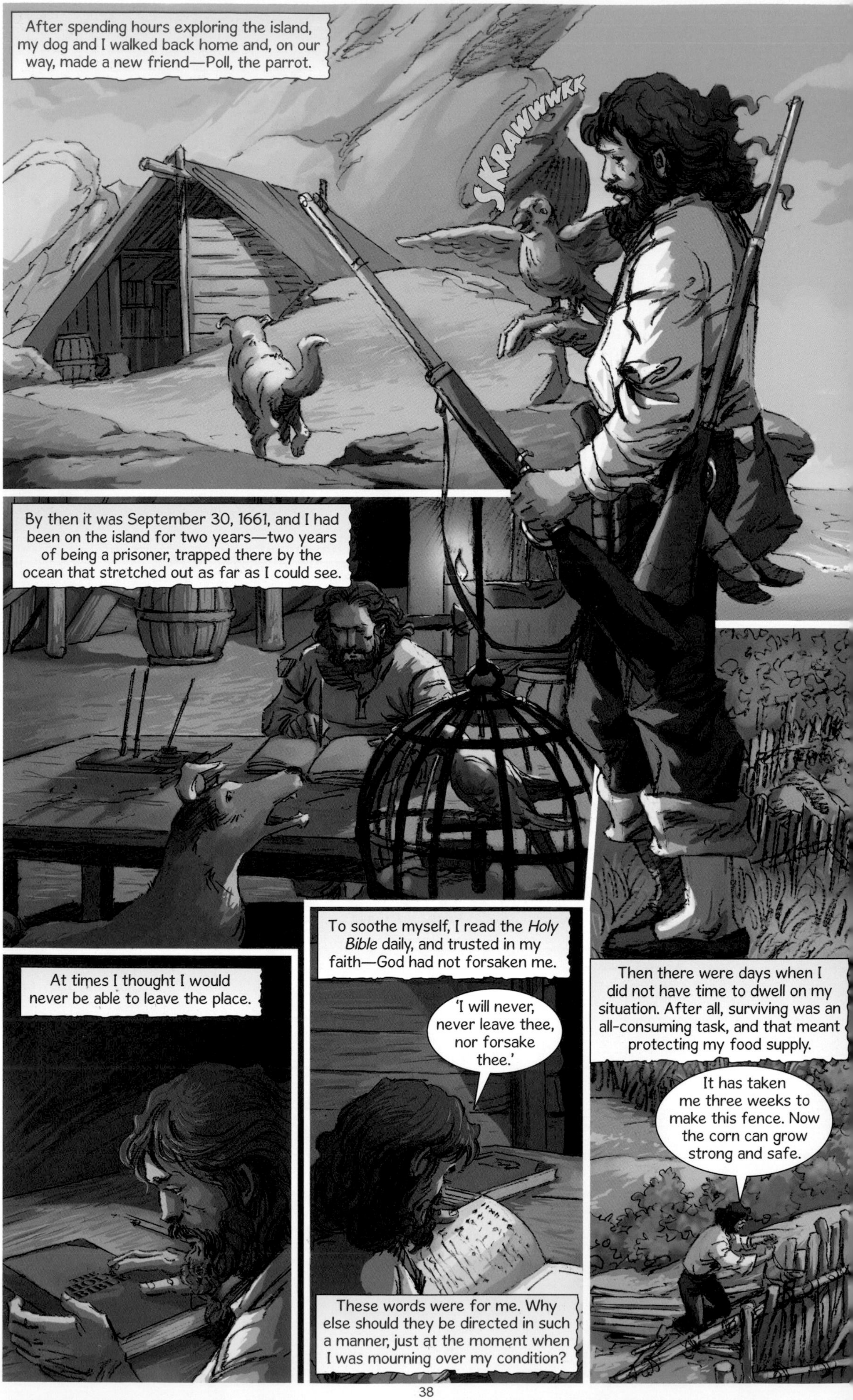
After spending hours exploring the island, my dog and I walked back home and, on our way, made a new friend—Poll, the parrot.
SKRAWWWKK
By then it was September 30, 1661, and I had been on the island for two years—two years of being a prisoner, trapped there by the ocean that stretched out as far as I could see.
At times I thought I would never be able to leave the place.
To soothe myself, I read the *Holy Bible* daily, and trusted in my faith—God had not forsaken me.
'I will never, never leave thee, nor forsake thee.'
These words were for me. Why else should they be directed in such a manner, just at the moment when I was mourning over my condition?
Then there were days when I did not have time to dwell on my situation. After all, surviving was an all-consuming task, and that meant protecting my food supply.
It has taken me three weeks to make this fence. Now the corn can grow strong and safe.

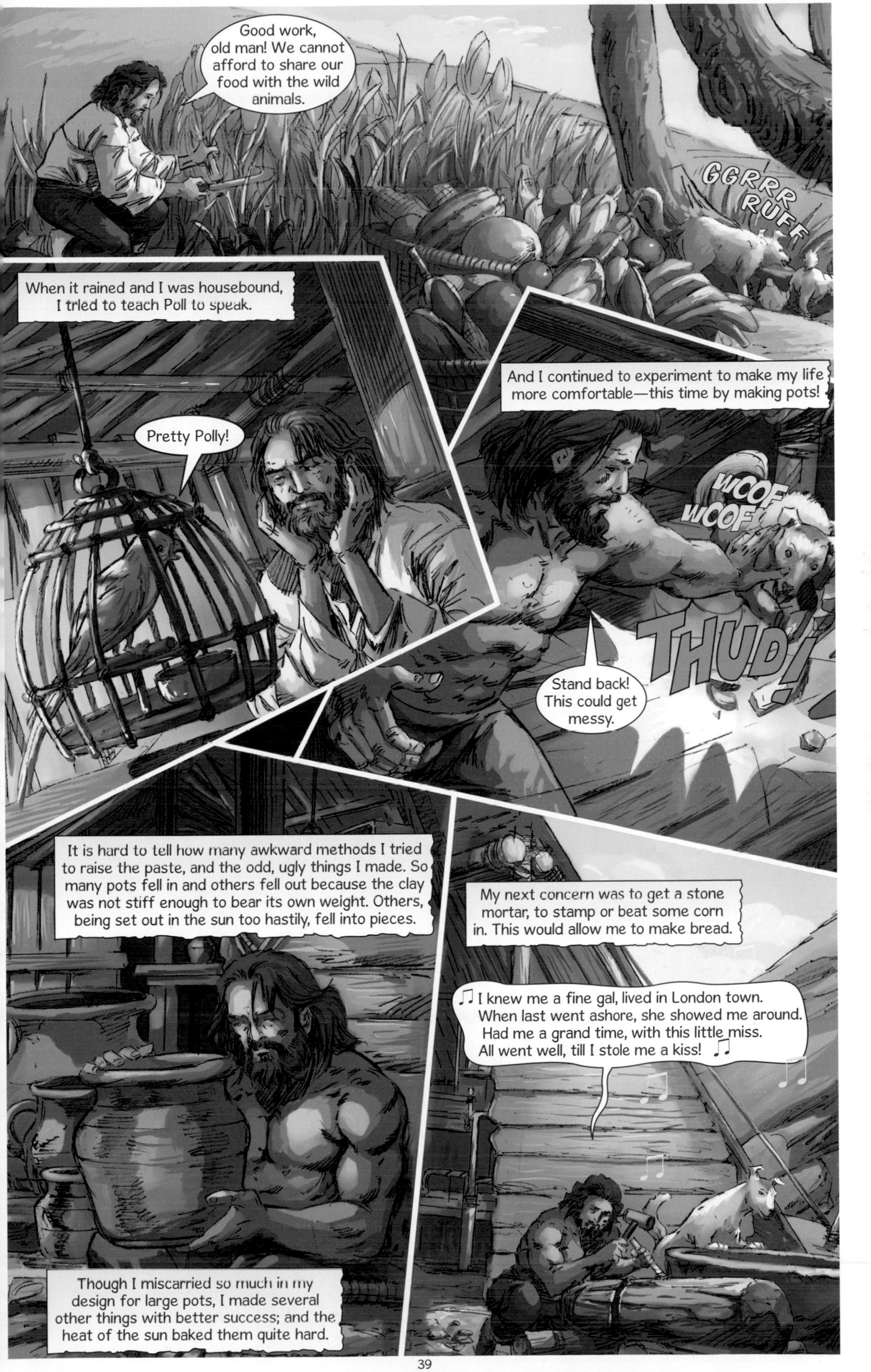
Good work, old man! We cannot afford to share our food with the wild animals.
GGRRRR RUFF
When it rained and I was housebound, I tried to teach Poll to speak.
Pretty Polly!
And I continued to experiment to make my life more comfortable—this time by making pots!
WOOF WOOF
THUD!
Stand back! This could get messy.
It is hard to tell how many awkward methods I tried to raise the paste, and the odd, ugly things I made. So many pots fell in and others fell out because the clay was not stiff enough to bear its own weight. Others, being set out in the sun too hastily, fell into pieces.
Though I miscarried so much in my design for large pots, I made several other things with better success; and the heat of the sun baked them quite hard.
My next concern was to get a stone mortar, to stamp or beat some corn in. This would allow me to make bread.
♫ I knew me a fine gal, lived in London town. When last went ashore, she showed me around. Had me a grand time, with this little miss. All went well, till I stole me a kiss! ♫

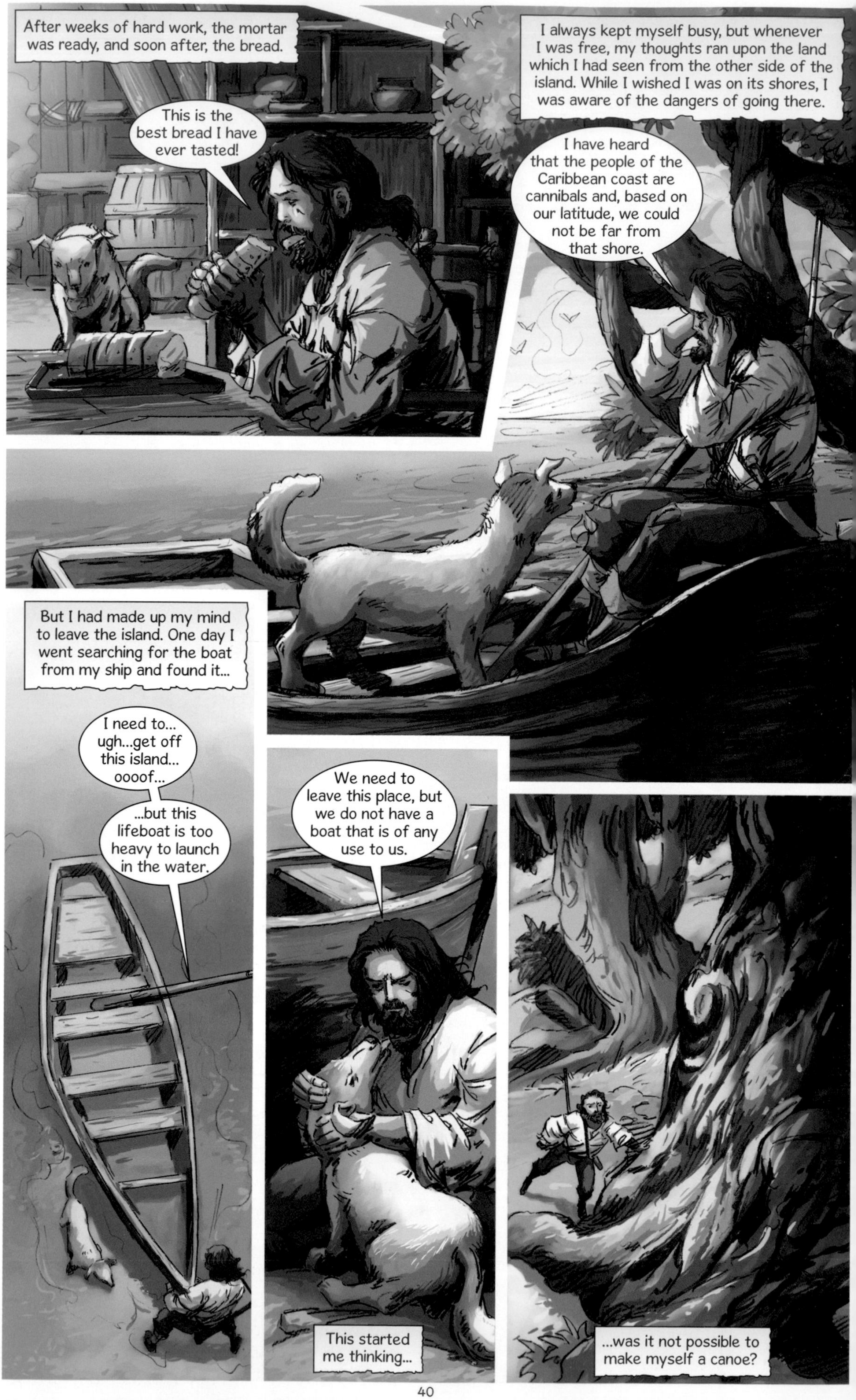
After weeks of hard work, the mortar was ready, and soon after, the bread.
This is the best bread I have ever tasted!
I always kept myself busy, but whenever I was free, my thoughts ran upon the land which I had seen from the other side of the island. While I wished I was on its shores, I was aware of the dangers of going there.
I have heard that the people of the Caribbean coast are cannibals and, based on our latitude, we could not be far from that shore.
But I had made up my mind to leave the island. One day I went searching for the boat from my ship and found it...
I need to... ugh...get off this island... oooof...
...but this lifeboat is too heavy to launch in the water.
We need to leave this place, but we do not have a boat that is of any use to us.
This started me thinking...
...was it not possible to make myself a canoe?

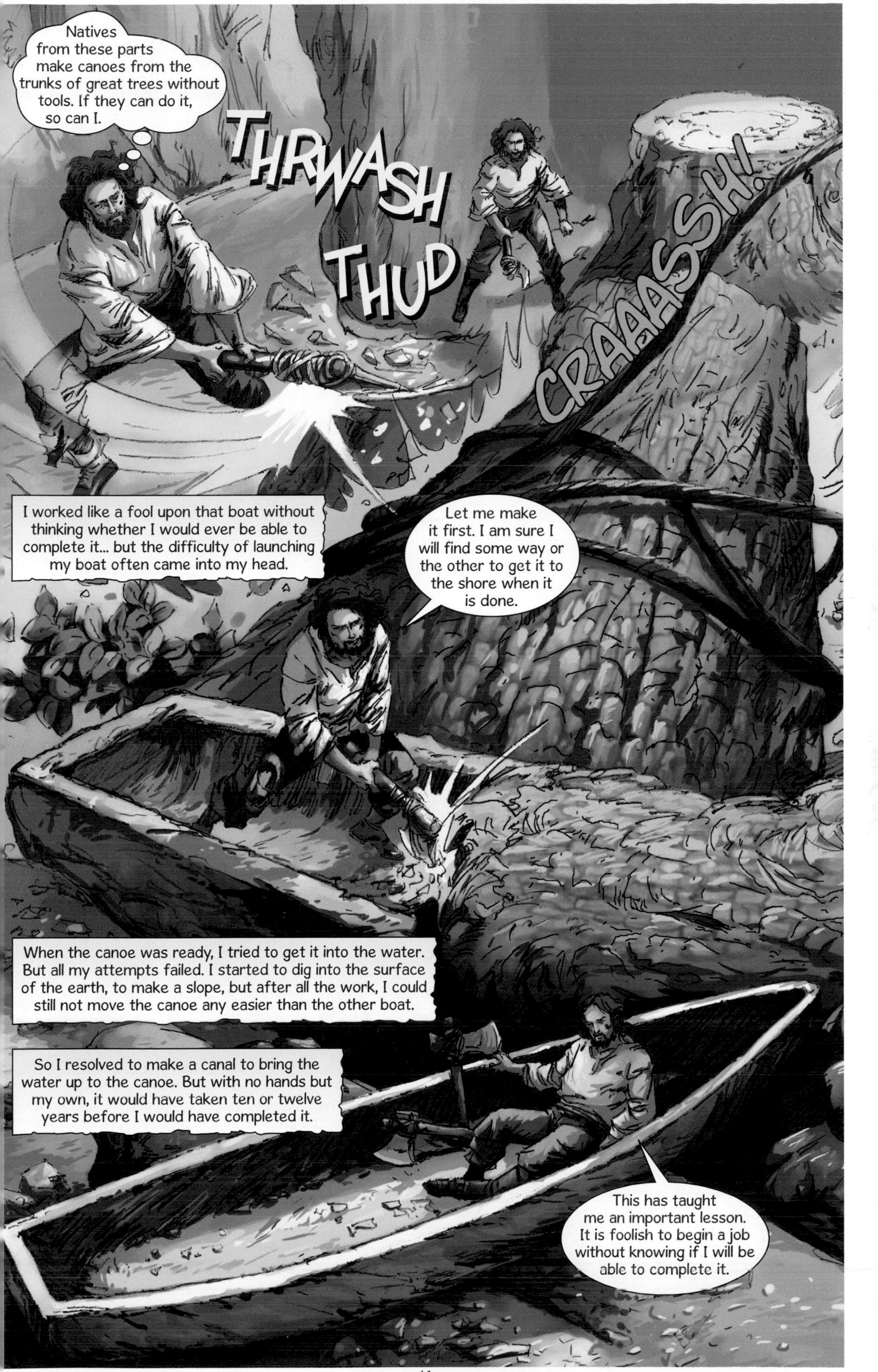
Natives from these parts make canoes from the trunks of great trees without tools. If they can do it, so can I.
THRWASH
THUD
CRAAASSH!
I worked like a fool upon that boat without thinking whether I would ever be able to complete it... but the difficulty of launching my boat often came into my head.
Let me make it first. I am sure I will find some way or the other to get it to the shore when it is done.
When the canoe was ready, I tried to get it into the water. But all my attempts failed. I started to dig into the surface of the earth, to make a slope, but after all the work, I could still not move the canoe any easier than the other boat.
So I resolved to make a canal to bring the water up to the canoe. But with no hands but my own, it would have taken ten or twelve years before I would have completed it.
This has taught me an important lesson. It is foolish to begin a job without knowing if I will be able to complete it.

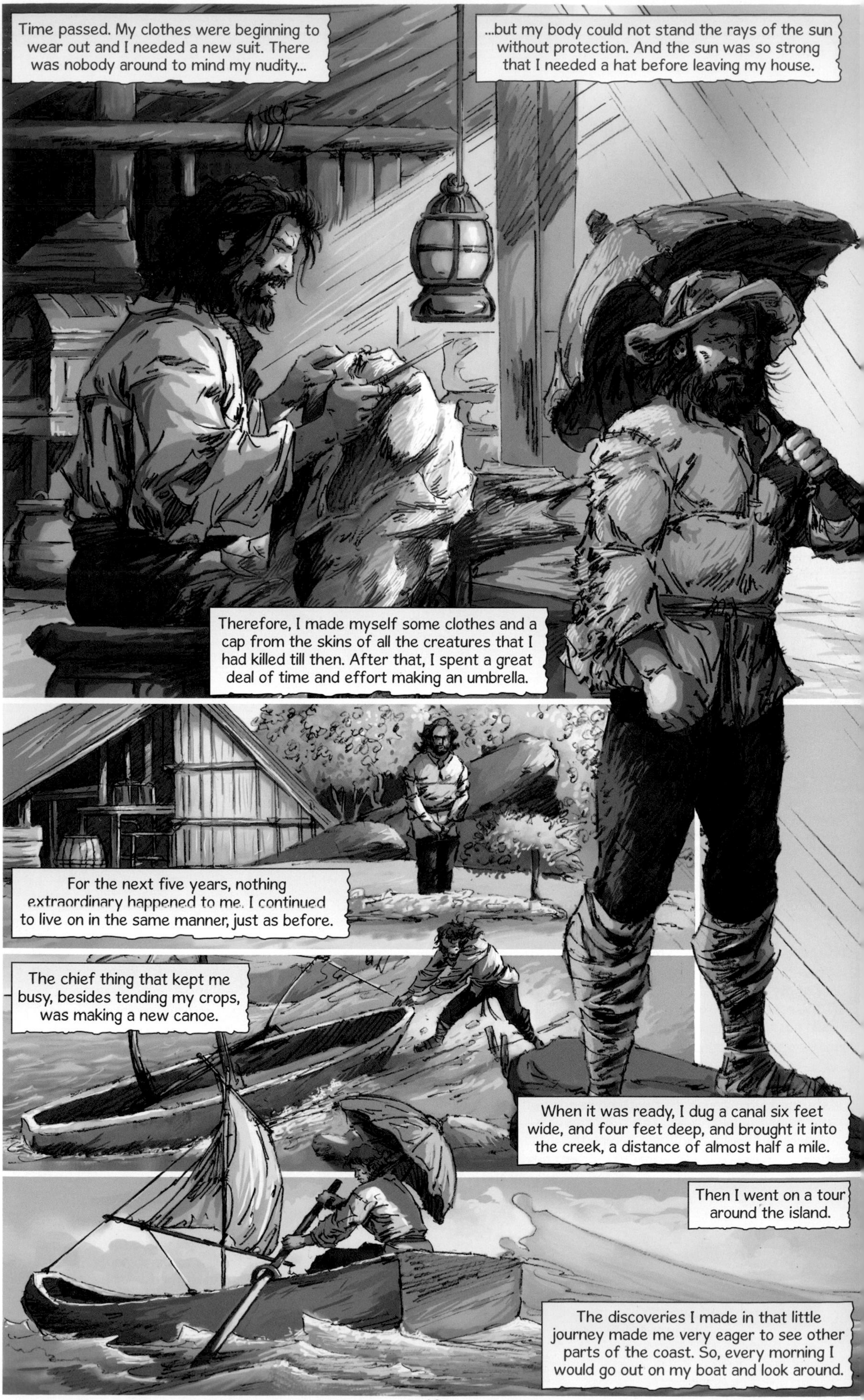
Time passed. My clothes were beginning to wear out and I needed a new suit. There was nobody around to mind my nudity...
...but my body could not stand the rays of the sun without protection. And the sun was so strong that I needed a hat before leaving my house.
Therefore, I made myself some clothes and a cap from the skins of all the creatures that I had killed till then. After that, I spent a great deal of time and effort making an umbrella.
For the next five years, nothing extraordinary happened to me. I continued to live on in the same manner, just as before.
The chief thing that kept me busy, besides tending my crops, was making a new canoe.
When it was ready, I dug a canal six feet wide, and four feet deep, and brought it into the creek, a distance of almost half a mile.
Then I went on a tour around the island.
The discoveries I made in that little journey made me very eager to see other parts of the coast. So, every morning I would go out on my boat and look around.

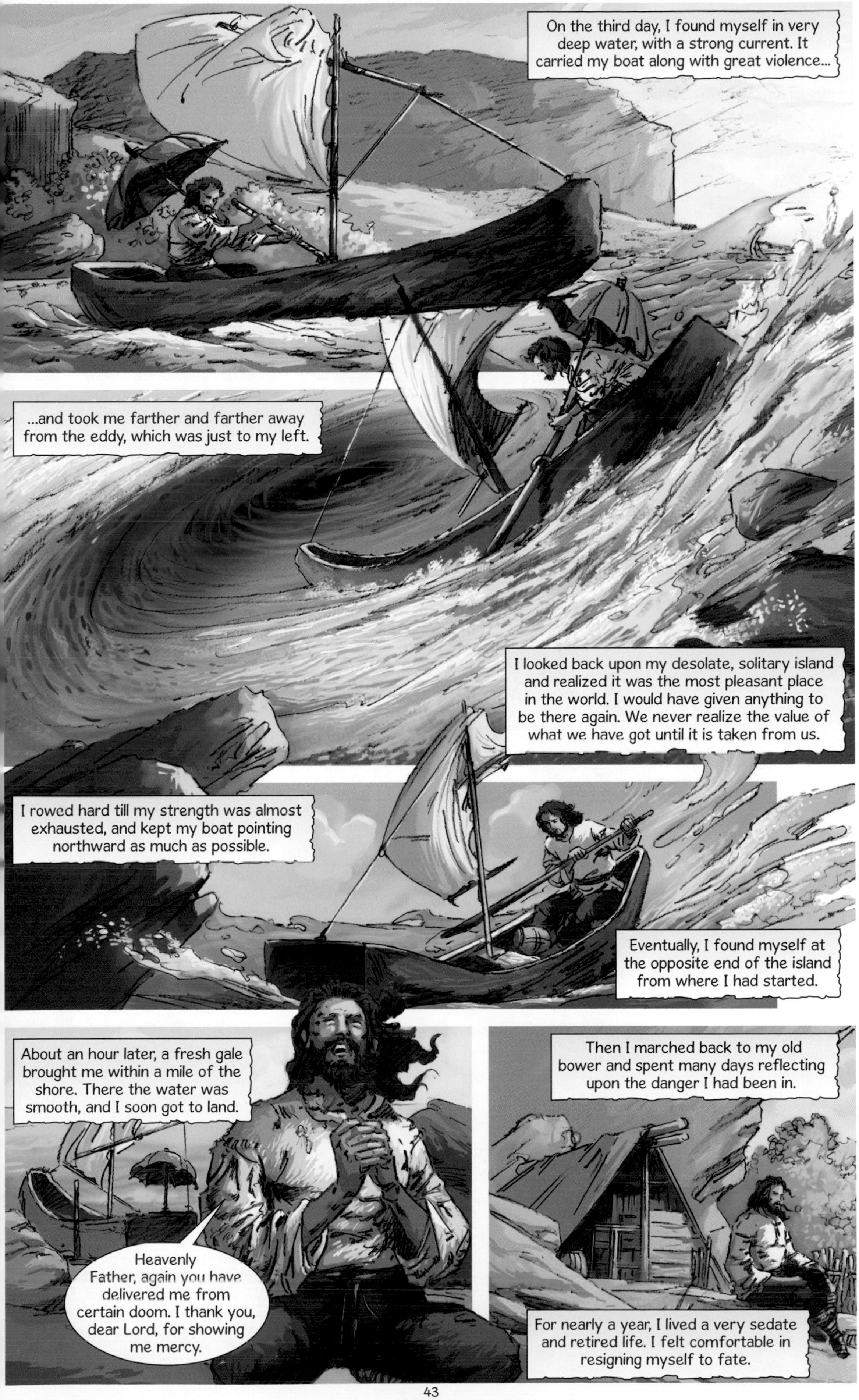
On the third day, I found myself in very deep water, with a strong current. It carried my boat along with great violence...
...and took me farther and farther away from the eddy, which was just to my left.
I looked back upon my desolate, solitary island and realized it was the most pleasant place in the world. I would have given anything to be there again. We never realize the value of what we have got until it is taken from us.
I rowed hard till my strength was almost exhausted, and kept my boat pointing northward as much as possible.
Eventually, I found myself at the opposite end of the island from where I had started.
About an hour later, a fresh gale brought me within a mile of the shore. There the water was smooth, and I soon got to land.
Heavenly Father, again you have delivered me from certain doom. I thank you, dear Lord, for showing me mercy.
Then I marched back to my old bower and spent many days reflecting upon the danger I had been in.
For nearly a year, I lived a very sedate and retired life. I felt comfortable in resigning myself to fate.

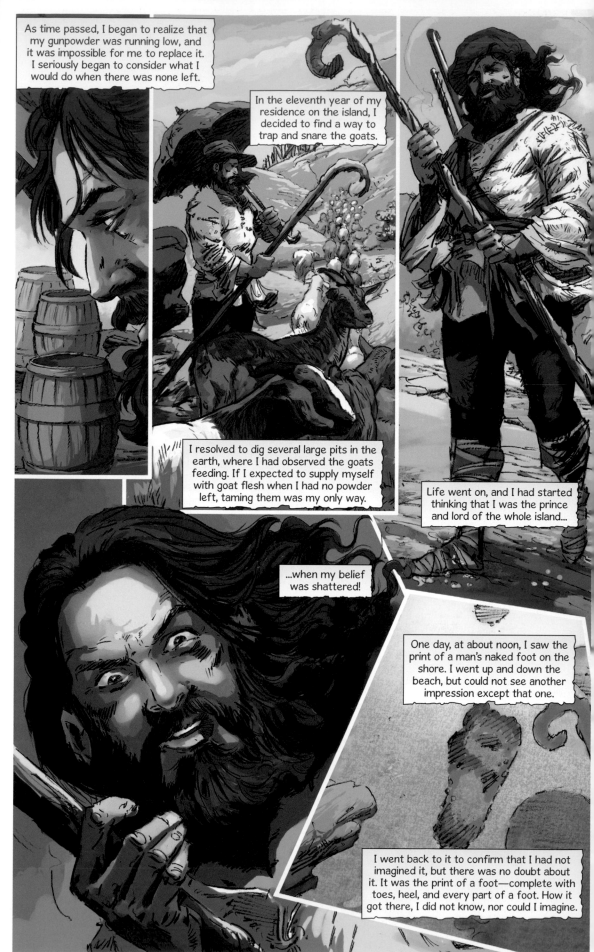

As time passed, I began to realize that my gunpowder was running low, and it was impossible for me to replace it. I seriously began to consider what I would do when there was none left.

In the eleventh year of my residence on the island, I decided to find a way to trap and snare the goats.

I resolved to dig several large pits in the earth, where I had observed the goats feeding. If I expected to supply myself with goat flesh when I had no powder left, taming them was my only way.

Life went on, and I had started thinking that I was the prince and lord of the whole island...

...when my belief was shattered!

One day, at about noon, I saw the print of a man's naked foot on the shore. I went up and down the beach, but could not see another impression except that one.

I went back to it to confirm that I had not imagined it, but there was no doubt about it. It was the print of a foot—complete with toes, heel, and every part of a foot. How it got there, I did not know, nor could I imagine.

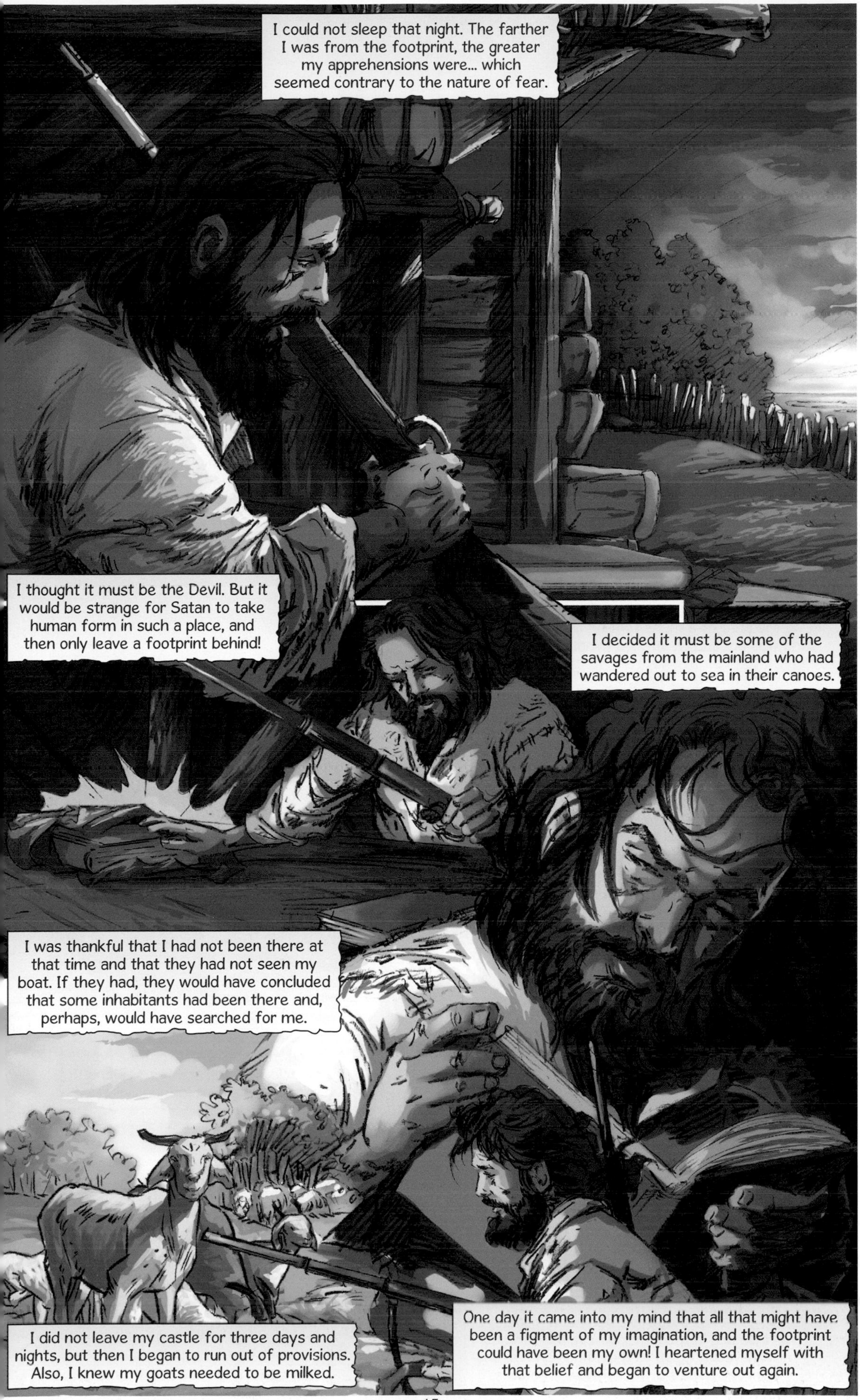
I could not sleep that night. The farther I was from the footprint, the greater my apprehensions were... which seemed contrary to the nature of fear.
I thought it must be the Devil. But it would be strange for Satan to take human form in such a place, and then only leave a footprint behind!
I decided it must be some of the savages from the mainland who had wandered out to sea in their canoes.
I was thankful that I had not been there at that time and that they had not seen my boat. If they had, they would have concluded that some inhabitants had been there and, perhaps, would have searched for me.
I did not leave my castle for three days and nights, but then I began to run out of provisions. Also, I knew my goats needed to be milked.
One day it came into my mind that all that might have been a figment of my imagination, and the footprint could have been my own! I heartened myself with that belief and began to venture out again.

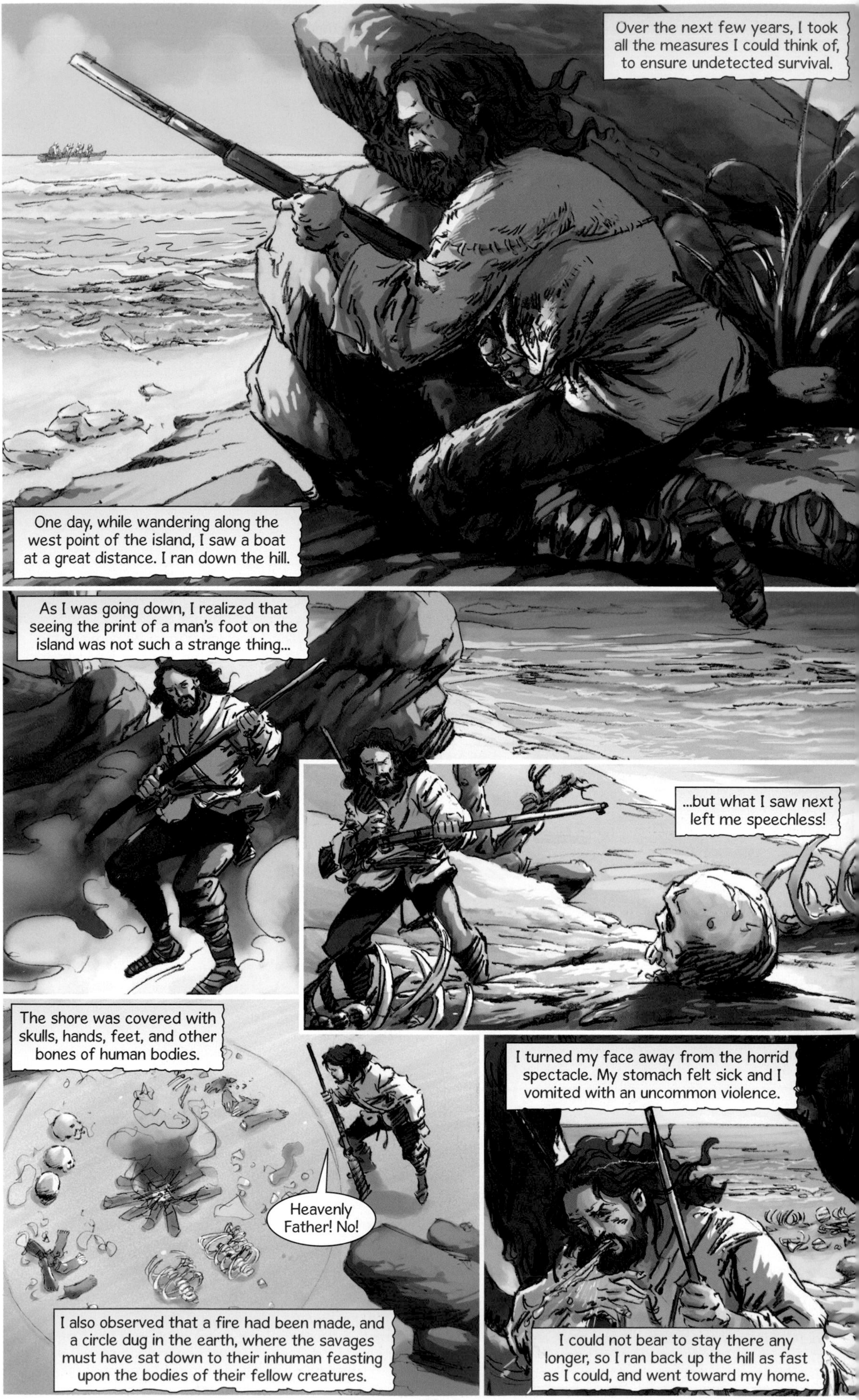
Over the next few years, I took all the measures I could think of, to ensure undetected survival.
One day, while wandering along the west point of the island, I saw a boat at a great distance. I ran down the hill.
As I was going down, I realized that seeing the print of a man's foot on the island was not such a strange thing...
...but what I saw next left me speechless!
The shore was covered with skulls, hands, feet, and other bones of human bodies.
Heavenly Father! No!
I also observed that a fire had been made, and a circle dug in the earth, where the savages must have sat down to their inhuman feasting upon the bodies of their fellow creatures.
I turned my face away from the horrid spectacle. My stomach felt sick and I vomited with an uncommon violence.
I could not bear to stay there any longer, so I ran back up the hill as fast as I could, and went toward my home.

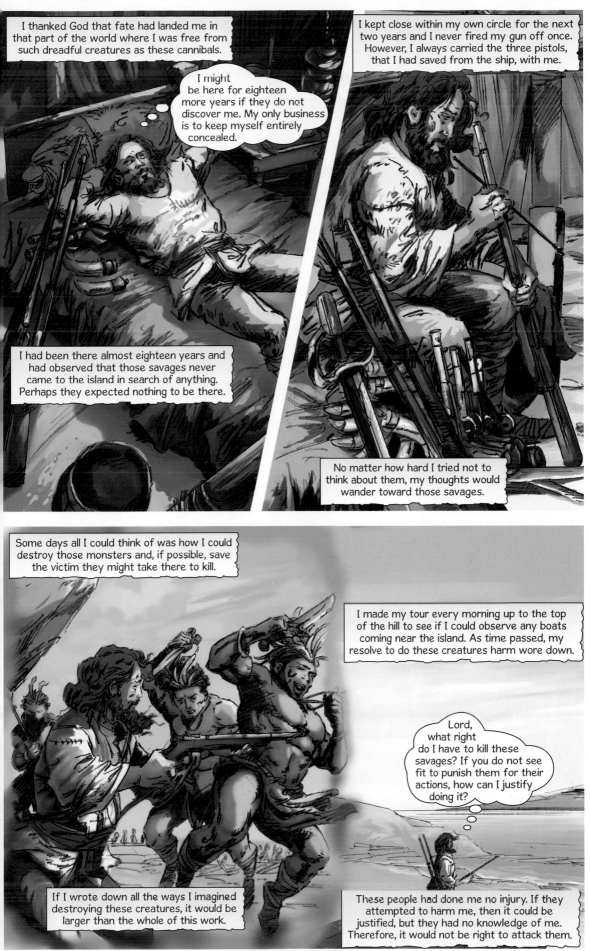

I thanked God that fate had landed me in that part of the world where I was free from such dreadful creatures as these cannibals.

I might be here for eighteen more years if they do not discover me. My only business is to keep myself entirely concealed.

I had been there almost eighteen years and had observed that those savages never came to the island in search of anything. Perhaps they expected nothing to be there.

I kept close within my own circle for the next two years and I never fired my gun off once. However, I always carried the three pistols, that I had saved from the ship, with me.

No matter how hard I tried not to think about them, my thoughts would wander toward those savages.

Some days all I could think of was how I could destroy those monsters and, if possible, save the victim they might take there to kill.

I made my tour every morning up to the top of the hill to see if I could observe any boats coming near the island. As time passed, my resolve to do these creatures harm wore down.

Lord, what right do I have to kill these savages? If you do not see fit to punish them for their actions, how can I justify doing it?

If I wrote down all the ways I imagined destroying these creatures, it would be larger than the whole of this work.

These people had done me no injury. If they attempted to harm me, then it could be justified, but they had no knowledge of me. Therefore, it would not be right to attack them.

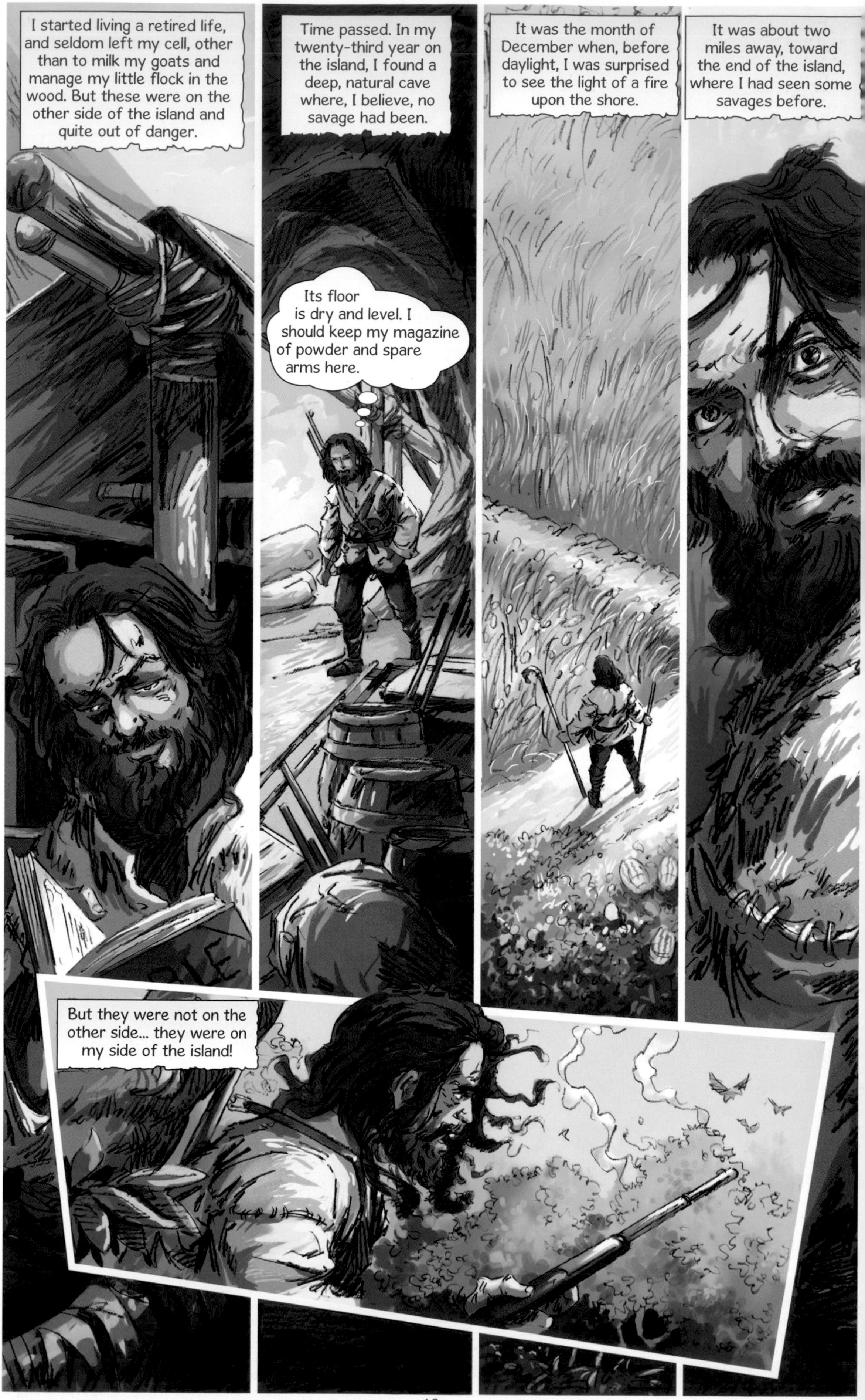
I started living a retired life, and seldom left my cell, other than to milk my goats and manage my little flock in the wood. But these were on the other side of the island and quite out of danger.
Time passed. In my twenty-third year on the island, I found a deep, natural cave where, I believe, no savage had been.
Its floor is dry and level. I should keep my magazine of powder and spare arms here.
It was the month of December when, before daylight, I was surprised to see the light of a fire upon the shore.
It was about two miles away, toward the end of the island, where I had seen some savages before.
But they were not on the other side... they were on my side of the island!

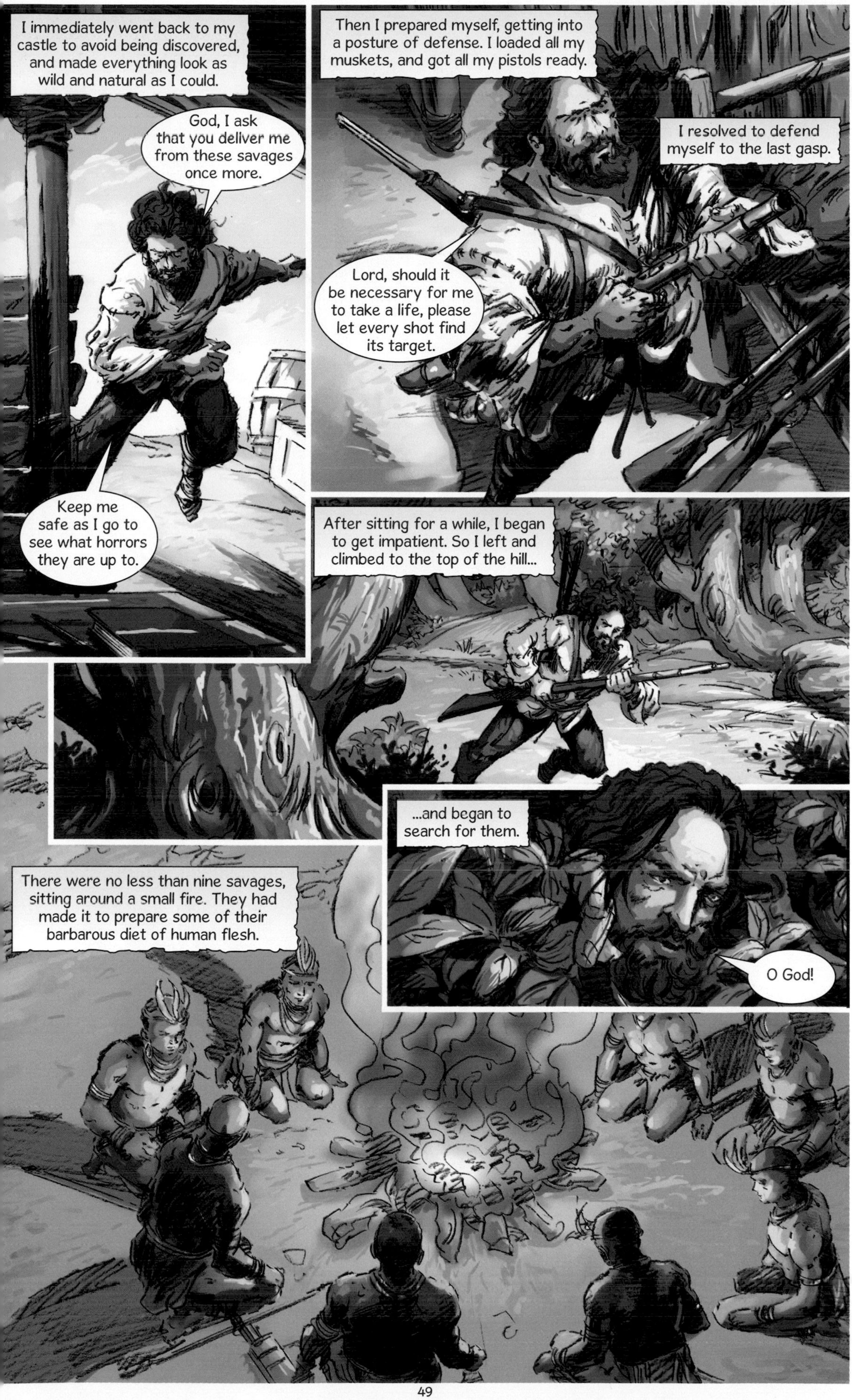
I immediately went back to my castle to avoid being discovered, and made everything look as wild and natural as I could.
God, I ask that you deliver me from these savages once more.
Keep me safe as I go to see what horrors they are up to.
Then I prepared myself, getting into a posture of defense. I loaded all my muskets, and got all my pistols ready.
I resolved to defend myself to the last gasp.
Lord, should it be necessary for me to take a life, please let every shot find its target.
After sitting for a while, I began to get impatient. So I left and climbed to the top of the hill...
...and began to search for them.
O God!
There were no less than nine savages, sitting around a small fire. They had made it to prepare some of their barbarous diet of human flesh.

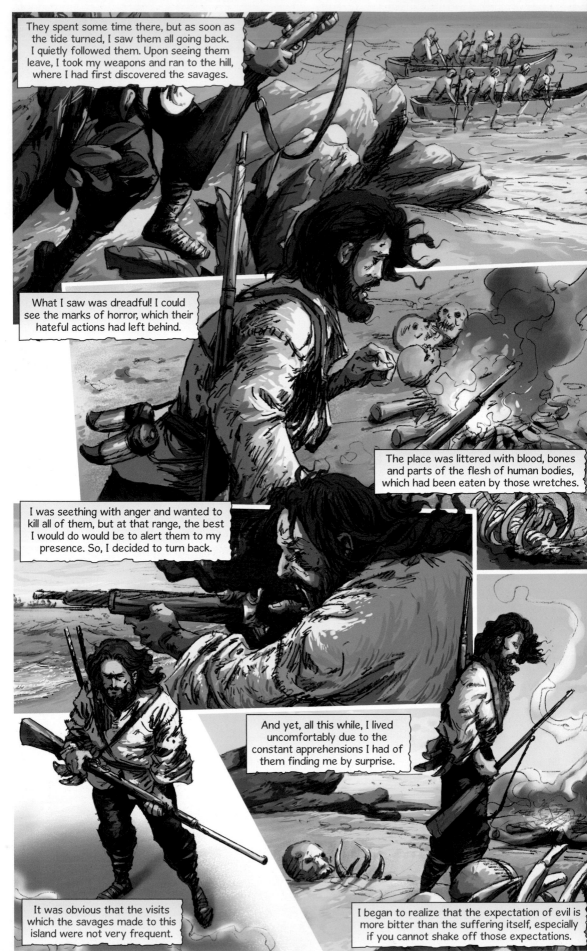

They spent some time there, but as soon as the tide turned, I saw them all going back. I quietly followed them. Upon seeing them leave, I took my weapons and ran to the hill, where I had first discovered the savages.

What I saw was dreadful! I could see the marks of horror, which their hateful actions had left behind.

The place was littered with blood, bones and parts of the flesh of human bodies, which had been eaten by those wretches.

I was seething with anger and wanted to kill all of them, but at that range, the best I would do would be to alert them to my presence. So, I decided to turn back.

And yet, all this while, I lived uncomfortably due to the constant apprehensions I had of them finding me by surprise.

It was obvious that the visits which the savages made to this island were not very frequent.

I began to realize that the expectation of evil is more bitter than the suffering itself, especially if you cannot shake off those expectations.

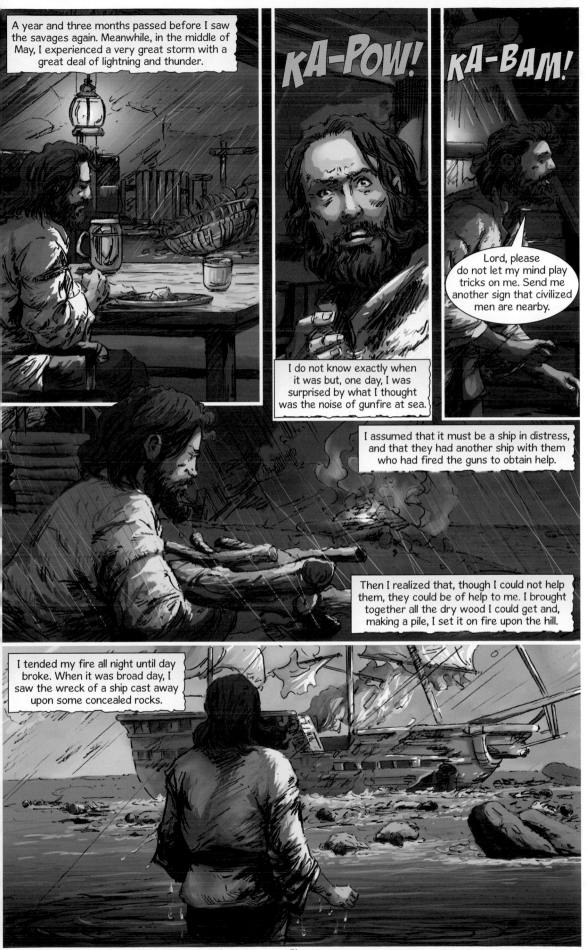

A year and three months passed before I saw the savages again. Meanwhile, in the middle of May, I experienced a very great storm with a great deal of lightning and thunder.

KA-POW!

KA-BAM!

Lord, please do not let my mind play tricks on me. Send me another sign that civilized men are nearby.

I do not know exactly when it was but, one day, I was surprised by what I thought was the noise of gunfire at sea.

I assumed that it must be a ship in distress, and that they had another ship with them who had fired the guns to obtain help.

Then I realized that, though I could not help them, they could be of help to me. I brought together all the dry wood I could get and, making a pile, I set it on fire upon the hill.

I tended my fire all night until day broke. When it was broad day, I saw the wreck of a ship cast away upon some concealed rocks.

Desperate for supplies, and hoping for a companion, I set sail toward the ship.

The fate of those who had been on board gave me more and more reason to thank God, who had provided for me in my desolate condition.

As for the dead, I could do no more than look upon the misery of these poor men, and pity them.

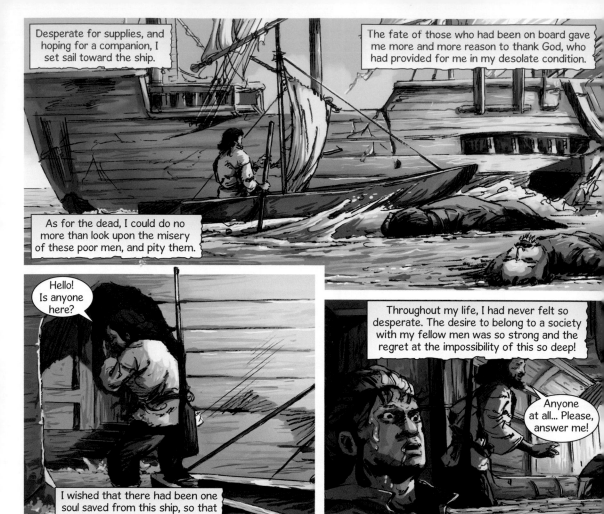

Hello! Is anyone here?

I wished that there had been one soul saved from this ship, so that I might have had a companion.

Throughout my life, I had never felt so desperate. The desire to belong to a society with my fellow men was so strong and the regret at the impossibility of this so deep!

Anyone at all... Please, answer me!

In the staterooms, I found some items that had survived the storm, including some rum, a fire shovel and tongs, brass kettles, and a grid iron.

Most importantly, I discovered a powder horn with four pounds of powder.

Upon further examination, I also found several shirts, handkerchiefs and neckcloths that were most welcomed. I resolved to store these goods in my cave and not carry them home.

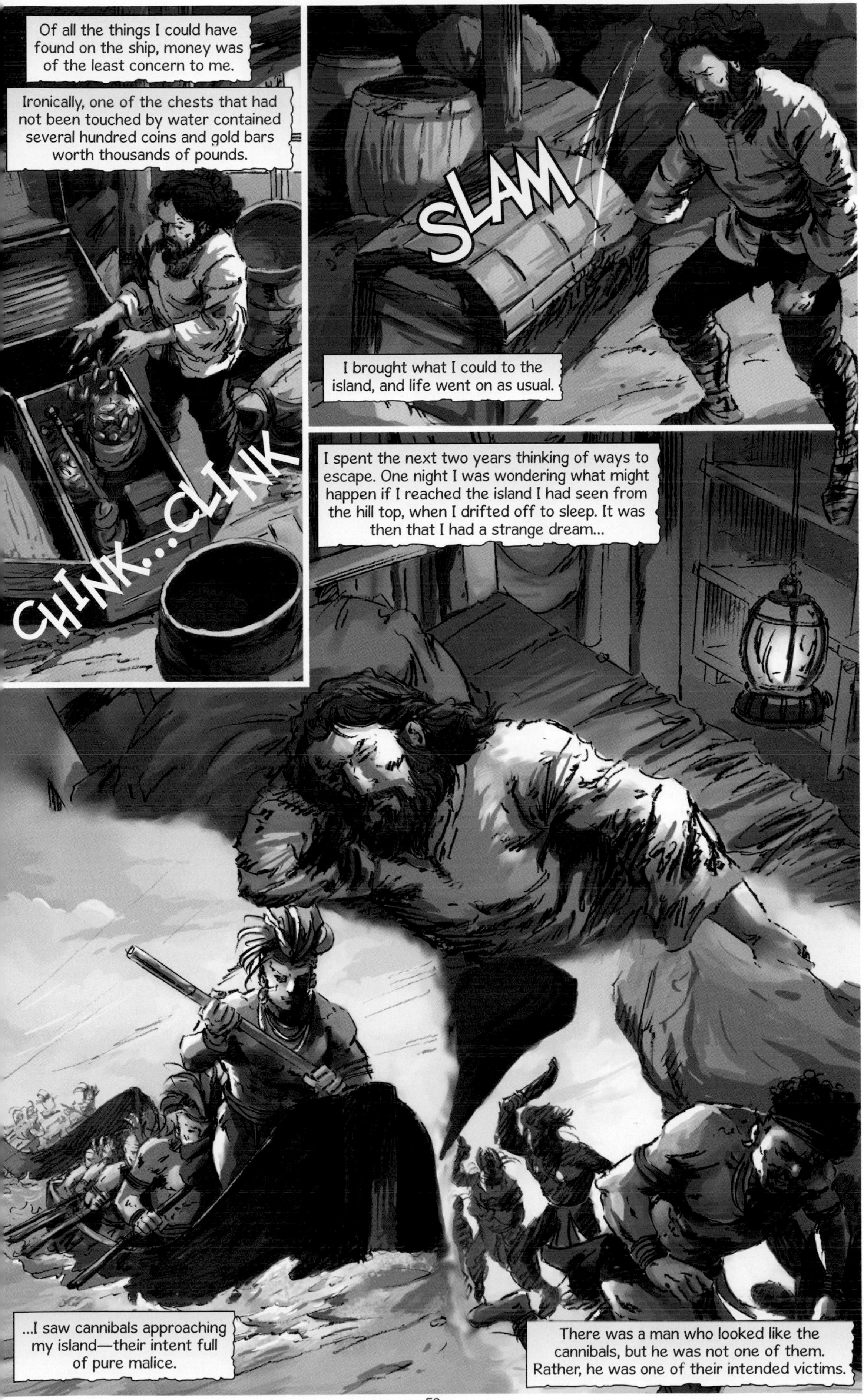
Of all the things I could have found on the ship, money was of the least concern to me.
Ironically, one of the chests that had not been touched by water contained several hundred coins and gold bars worth thousands of pounds.
CHINK...CLINK
SLAM
I brought what I could to the island, and life went on as usual.
I spent the next two years thinking of ways to escape. One night I was wondering what might happen if I reached the island I had seen from the hill top, when I drifted off to sleep. It was then that I had a strange dream...
...I saw cannibals approaching my island—their intent full of pure malice.
There was a man who looked like the cannibals, but he was not one of them. Rather, he was one of their intended victims.

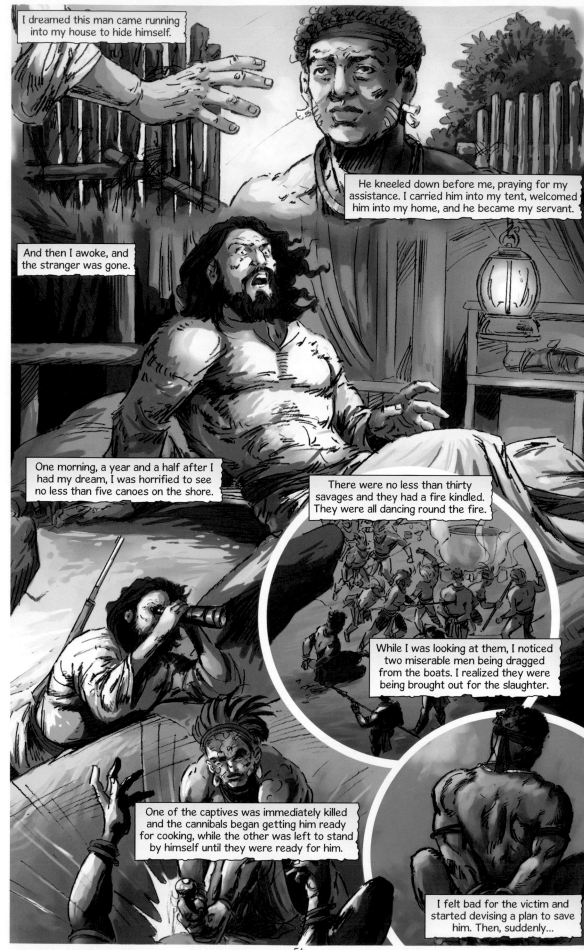

I dreamed this man came running into my house to hide himself.

He kneeled down before me, praying for my assistance. I carried him into my tent, welcomed him into my home, and he became my servant.

And then I awoke, and the stranger was gone.

One morning, a year and a half after I had my dream, I was horrified to see no less than five canoes on the shore.

There were no less than thirty savages and they had a fire kindled. They were all dancing round the fire.

While I was looking at them, I noticed two miserable men being dragged from the boats. I realized they were being brought out for the slaughter.

One of the captives was immediately killed and the cannibals began getting him ready for cooking, while the other was left to stand by himself until they were ready for him.

I felt bad for the victim and started devising a plan to save him. Then, suddenly...

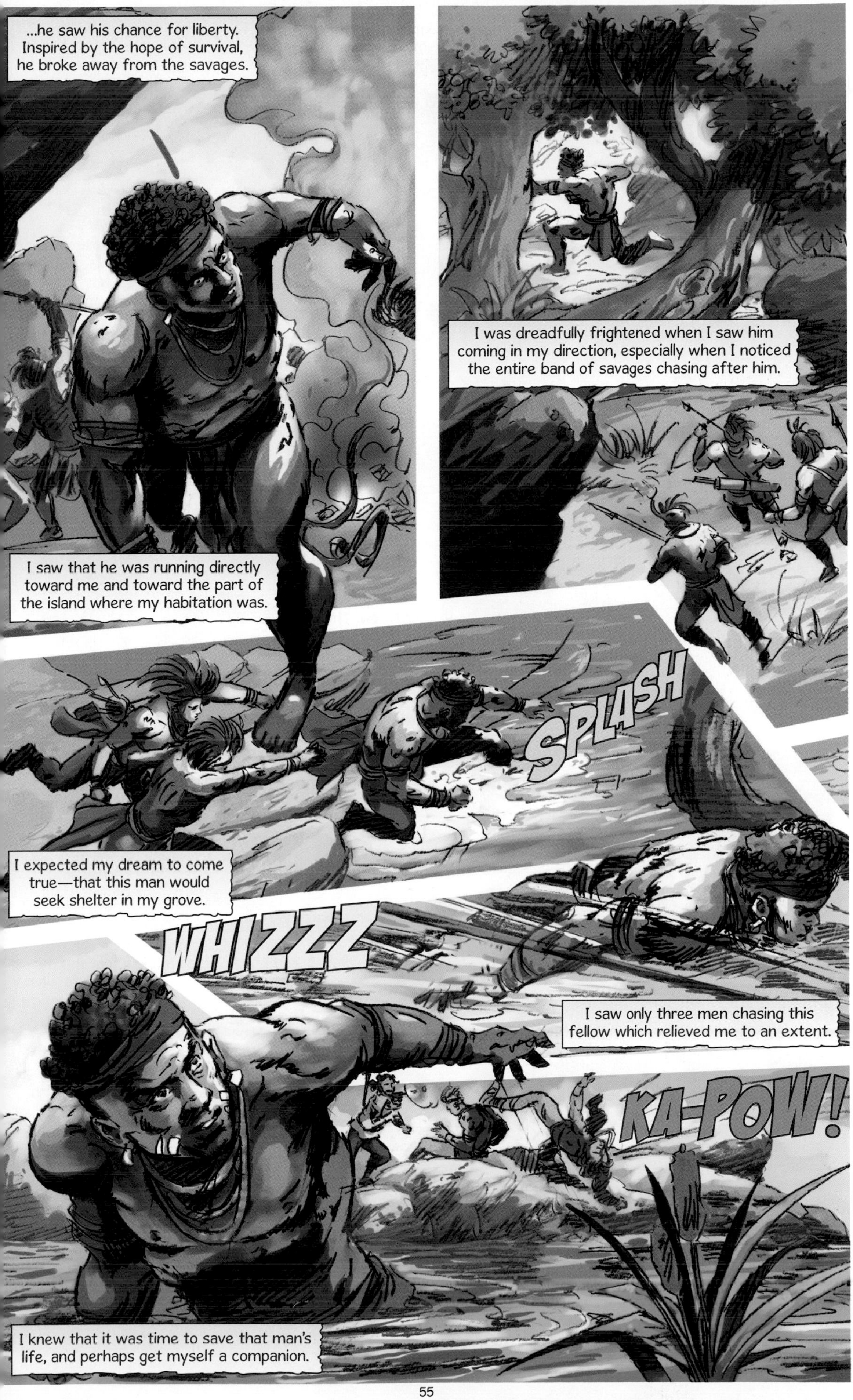
...he saw his chance for liberty. Inspired by the hope of survival, he broke away from the savages.
I was dreadfully frightened when I saw him coming in my direction, especially when I noticed the entire band of savages chasing after him.
I saw that he was running directly toward me and toward the part of the island where my habitation was.
SPLASH
I expected my dream to come true—that this man would seek shelter in my grove.
WHIZZZ
I saw only three men chasing this fellow which relieved me to an extent.
KA-POW!
I knew that it was time to save that man's life, and perhaps get myself a companion.

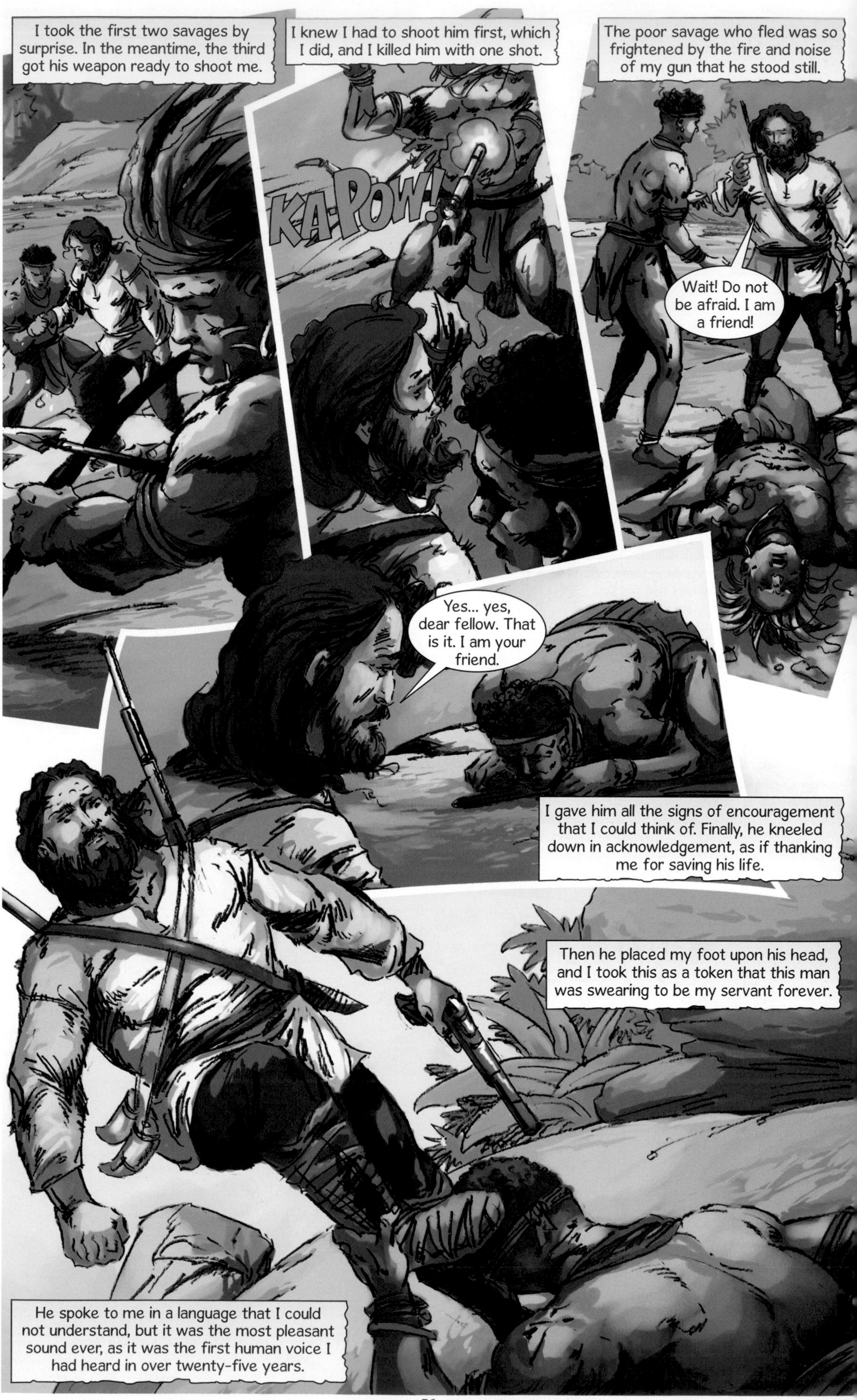
I took the first two savages by surprise. In the meantime, the third got his weapon ready to shoot me.
I knew I had to shoot him first, which I did, and I killed him with one shot.
KA-POW!
The poor savage who fled was so frightened by the fire and noise of my gun that he stood still.
Wait! Do not be afraid. I am a friend!
Yes... yes, dear fellow. That is it. I am your friend.
I gave him all the signs of encouragement that I could think of. Finally, he kneeled down in acknowledgement, as if thanking me for saving his life.
Then he placed my foot upon his head, and I took this as a token that this man was swearing to be my servant forever.
He spoke to me in a language that I could not understand, but it was the most pleasant sound ever, as it was the first human voice I had heard in over twenty-five years.

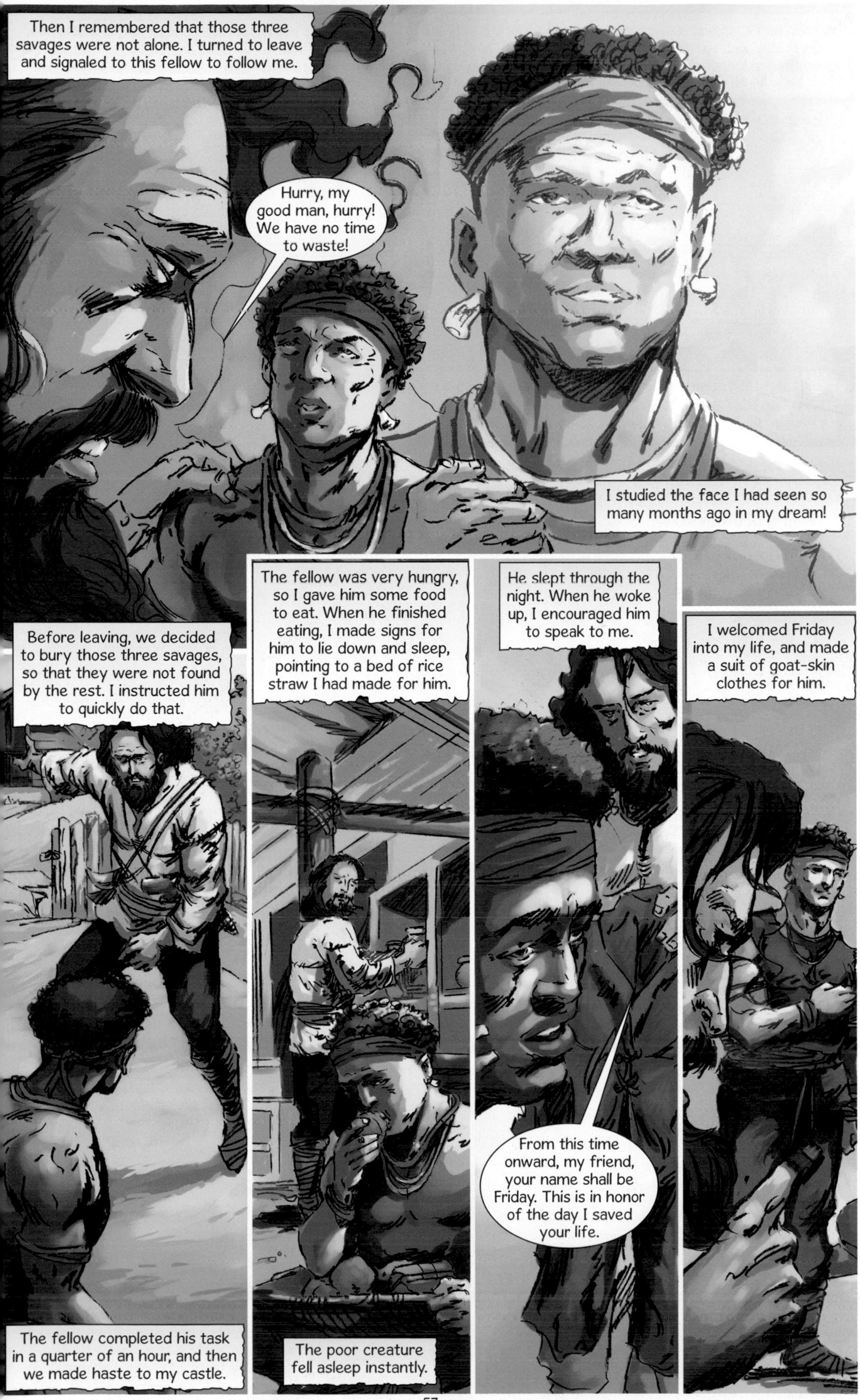
Then I remembered that those three savages were not alone. I turned to leave and signaled to this fellow to follow me.
Hurry, my good man, hurry! We have no time to waste!
I studied the face I had seen so many months ago in my dream!
Before leaving, we decided to bury those three savages, so that they were not found by the rest. I instructed him to quickly do that.
The fellow completed his task in a quarter of an hour, and then we made haste to my castle.
The fellow was very hungry, so I gave him some food to eat. When he finished eating, I made signs for him to lie down and sleep, pointing to a bed of rice straw I had made for him.
The poor creature fell asleep instantly.
He slept through the night. When he woke up, I encouraged him to speak to me.
From this time onward, my friend, your name shall be Friday. This is in honor of the day I saved your life.
I welcomed Friday into my life, and made a suit of goat-skin clothes for him.

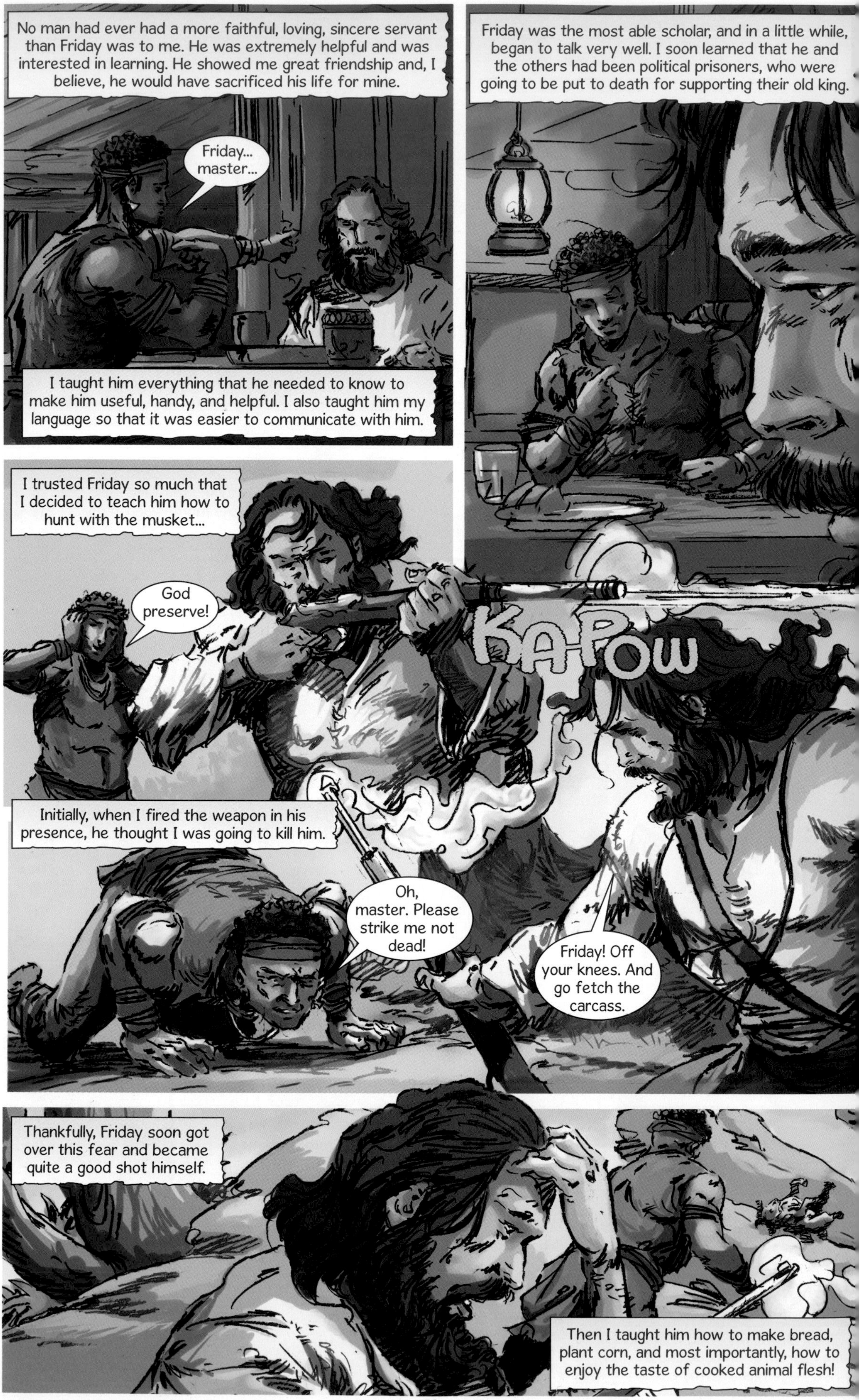
No man had ever had a more faithful, loving, sincere servant than Friday was to me. He was extremely helpful and was interested in learning. He showed me great friendship and, I believe, he would have sacrificed his life for mine.
Friday... master...
I taught him everything that he needed to know to make him useful, handy, and helpful. I also taught him my language so that it was easier to communicate with him.
Friday was the most able scholar, and in a little while, began to talk very well. I soon learned that he and the others had been political prisoners, who were going to be put to death for supporting their old king.
I trusted Friday so much that I decided to teach him how to hunt with the musket...
God preserve!
KA-POW
Initially, when I fired the weapon in his presence, he thought I was going to kill him.
Oh, master. Please strike me not dead!
Friday! Off your knees. And go fetch the carcass.
Thankfully, Friday soon got over this fear and became quite a good shot himself.
Then I taught him how to make bread, plant corn, and most importantly, how to enjoy the taste of cooked animal flesh!

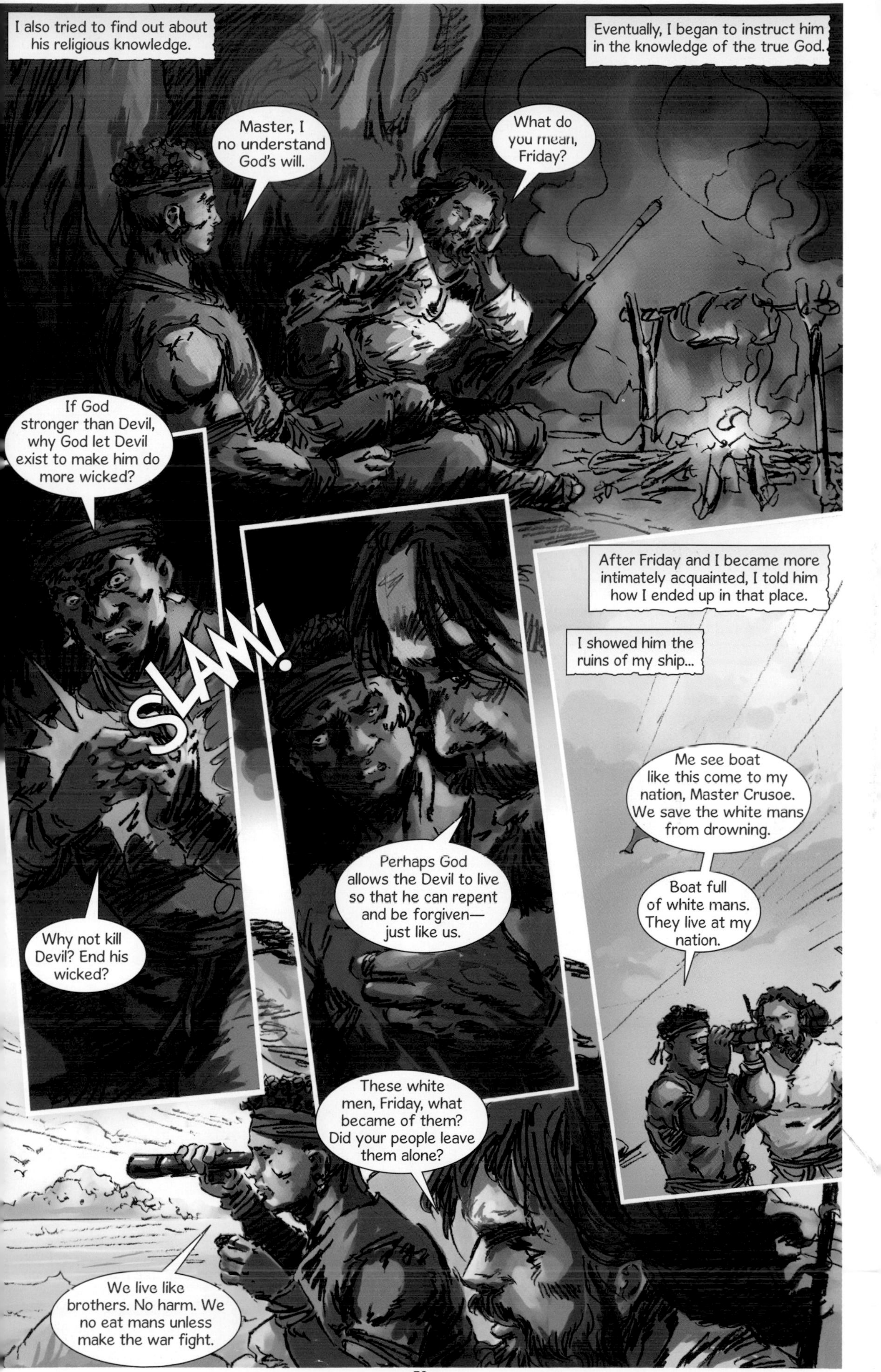
I also tried to find out about his religious knowledge.
Master, I no understand God's will.
What do you mean, Friday?
Eventually, I began to instruct him in the knowledge of the true God.
If God stronger than Devil, why God let Devil exist to make him do more wicked?
SLAM!
Why not kill Devil? End his wicked?
Perhaps God allows the Devil to live so that he can repent and be forgiven—just like us.
After Friday and I became more intimately acquainted, I told him how I ended up in that place.
I showed him the ruins of my ship...
Me see boat like this come to my nation, Master Crusoe. We save the white mans from drowning.
Boat full of white mans. They live at my nation.
These white men, Friday, what became of them? Did your people leave them alone?
We live like brothers. No harm. We no eat mans unless make the war fight.

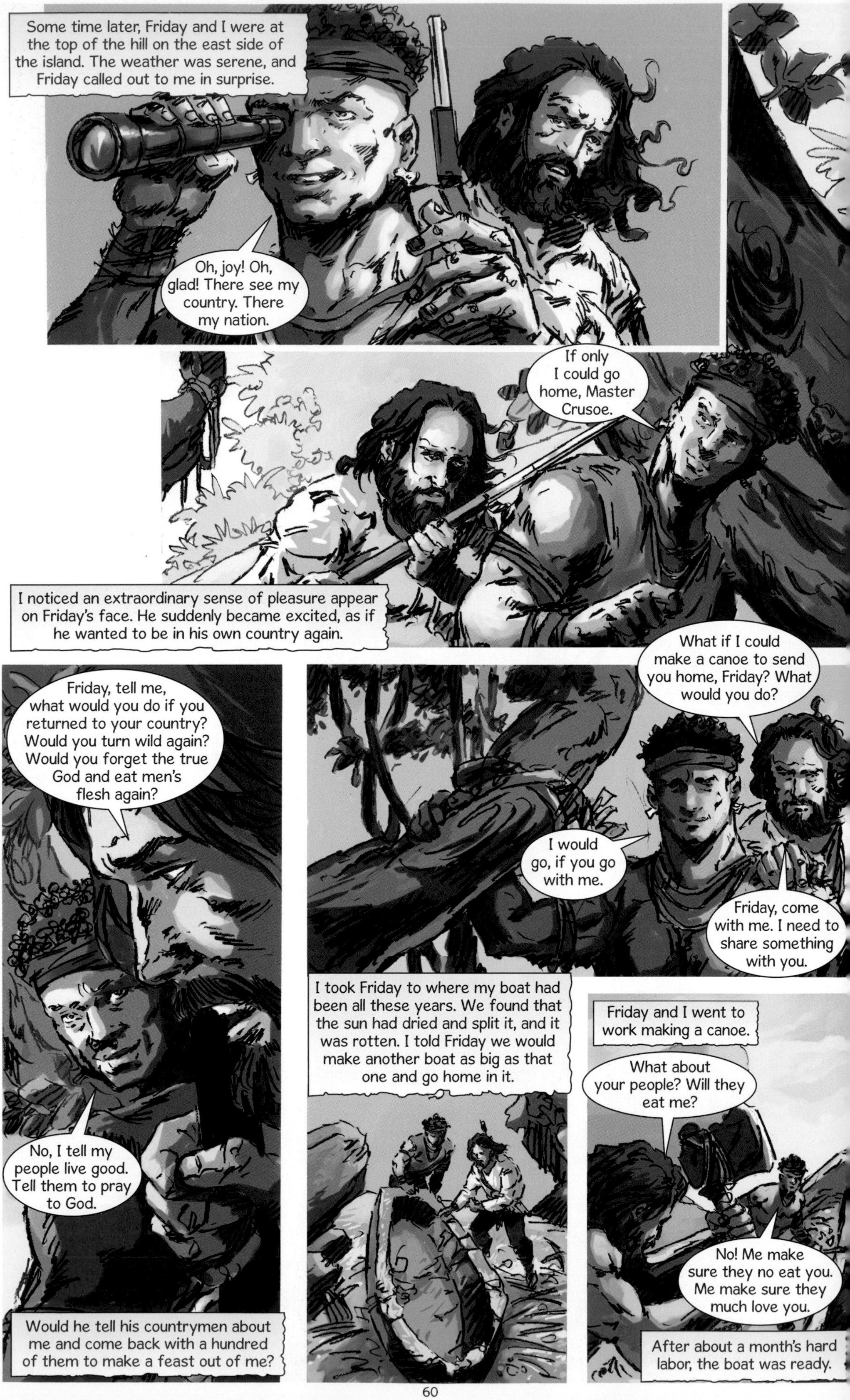

Some time later, Friday and I were at the top of the hill on the east side of the island. The weather was serene, and Friday called out to me in surprise.
Oh, joy! Oh, glad! There see my country. There my nation.
If only I could go home, Master Crusoe.
I noticed an extraordinary sense of pleasure appear on Friday's face. He suddenly became excited, as if he wanted to be in his own country again.
Friday, tell me, what would you do if you returned to your country? Would you turn wild again? Would you forget the true God and eat men's flesh again?
No, I tell my people live good. Tell them to pray to God.
Would he tell his countrymen about me and come back with a hundred of them to make a feast out of me?
What if I could make a canoe to send you home, Friday? What would you do?
I would go, if you go with me.
Friday, come with me. I need to share something with you.
I took Friday to where my boat had been all these years. We found that the sun had dried and split it, and it was rotten. I told Friday we would make another boat as big as that one and go home in it.
Friday and I went to work making a canoe.
What about your people? Will they eat me?
No! Me make sure they no eat you. Me make sure they much love you.
After about a month's hard labor, the boat was ready.

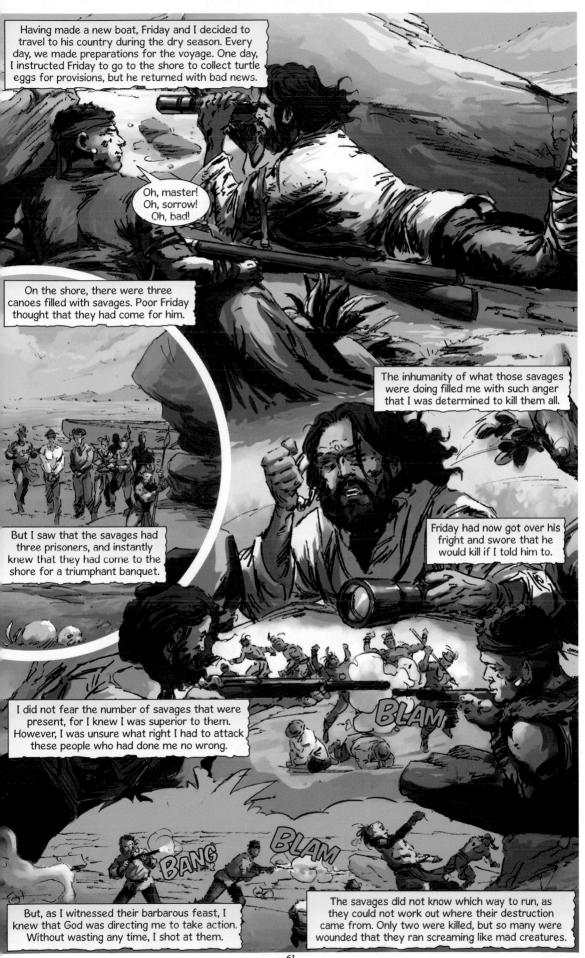

Having made a new boat, Friday and I decided to travel to his country during the dry season. Every day, we made preparations for the voyage. One day, I instructed Friday to go to the shore to collect turtle eggs for provisions, but he returned with bad news.

Oh, master!
Oh, sorrow!
Oh, bad!

On the shore, there were three canoes filled with savages. Poor Friday thought that they had come for him.

The inhumanity of what those savages were doing filled me with such anger that I was determined to kill them all.

But I saw that the savages had three prisoners, and instantly knew that they had come to the shore for a triumphant banquet.

Friday had now got over his fright and swore that he would kill if I told him to.

I did not fear the number of savages that were present, for I knew I was superior to them. However, I was unsure what right I had to attack these people who had done me no wrong.

BLAM

BANG

BLAM

But, as I witnessed their barbarous feast, I knew that God was directing me to take action. Without wasting any time, I shot at them.

The savages did not know which way to run, as they could not work out where their destruction came from. Only two were killed, but so many were wounded that they ran screaming like mad creatures.

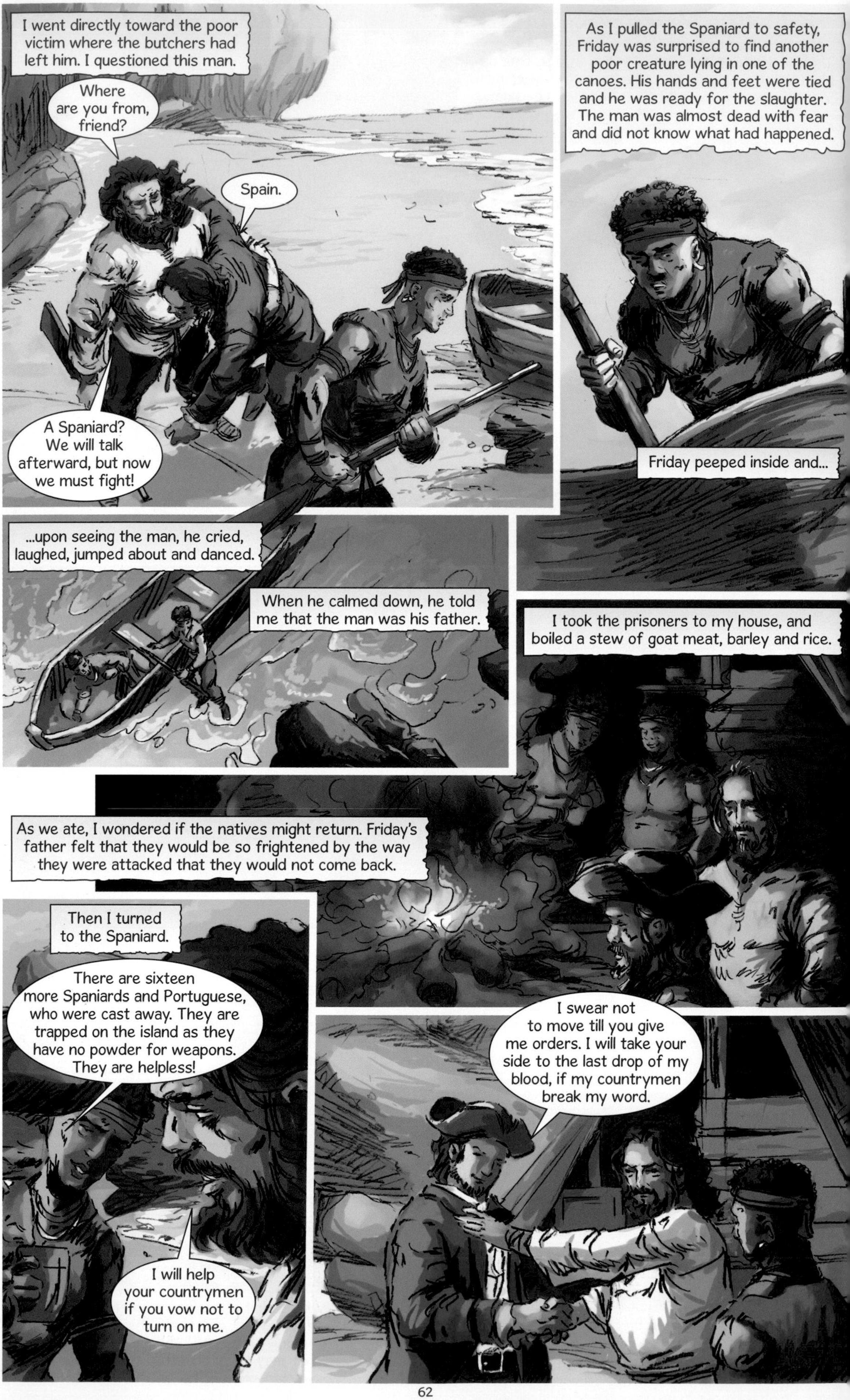
I went directly toward the poor victim where the butchers had left him. I questioned this man.
Where are you from, friend?
Spain.
A Spaniard? We will talk afterward, but now we must fight!
As I pulled the Spaniard to safety, Friday was surprised to find another poor creature lying in one of the canoes. His hands and feet were tied and he was ready for the slaughter. The man was almost dead with fear and did not know what had happened.
Friday peeped inside and...
...upon seeing the man, he cried, laughed, jumped about and danced.
When he calmed down, he told me that the man was his father.
I took the prisoners to my house, and boiled a stew of goat meat, barley and rice.
As we ate, I wondered if the natives might return. Friday's father felt that they would be so frightened by the way they were attacked that they would not come back.
Then I turned to the Spaniard.
There are sixteen more Spaniards and Portuguese, who were cast away. They are trapped on the island as they have no powder for weapons. They are helpless!
I will help your countrymen if you vow not to turn on me.
I swear not to move till you give me orders. I will take your side to the last drop of my blood, if my countrymen break my word.

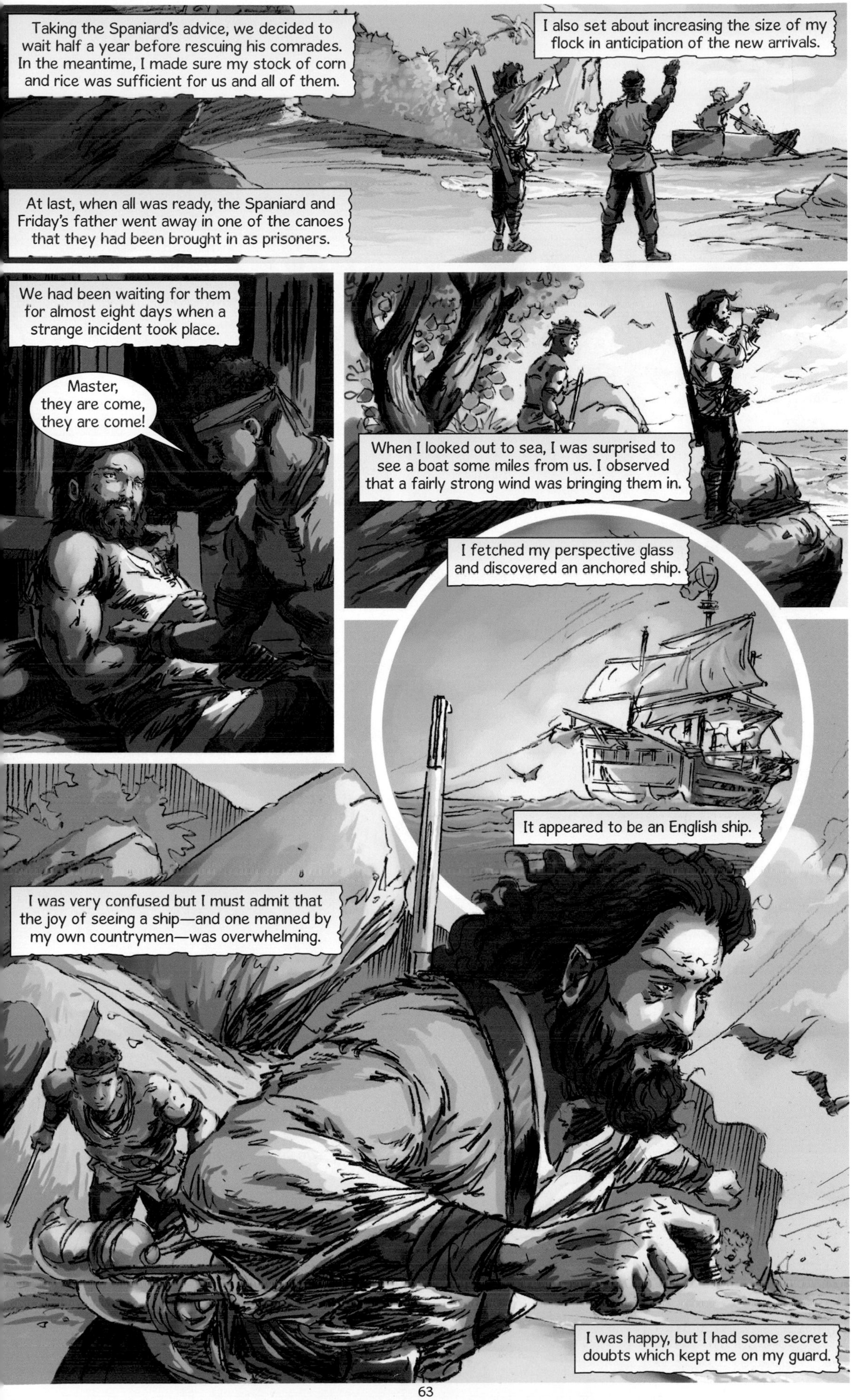
Taking the Spaniard's advice, we decided to wait half a year before rescuing his comrades. In the meantime, I made sure my stock of corn and rice was sufficient for us and all of them.
I also set about increasing the size of my flock in anticipation of the new arrivals.
At last, when all was ready, the Spaniard and Friday's father went away in one of the canoes that they had been brought in as prisoners.
We had been waiting for them for almost eight days when a strange incident took place.
Master, they are come, they are come!
When I looked out to sea, I was surprised to see a boat some miles from us. I observed that a fairly strong wind was bringing them in.
I fetched my perspective glass and discovered an anchored ship.
It appeared to be an English ship.
I was very confused but I must admit that the joy of seeing a ship—and one manned by my own countrymen—was overwhelming.
I was happy, but I had some secret doubts which kept me on my guard.

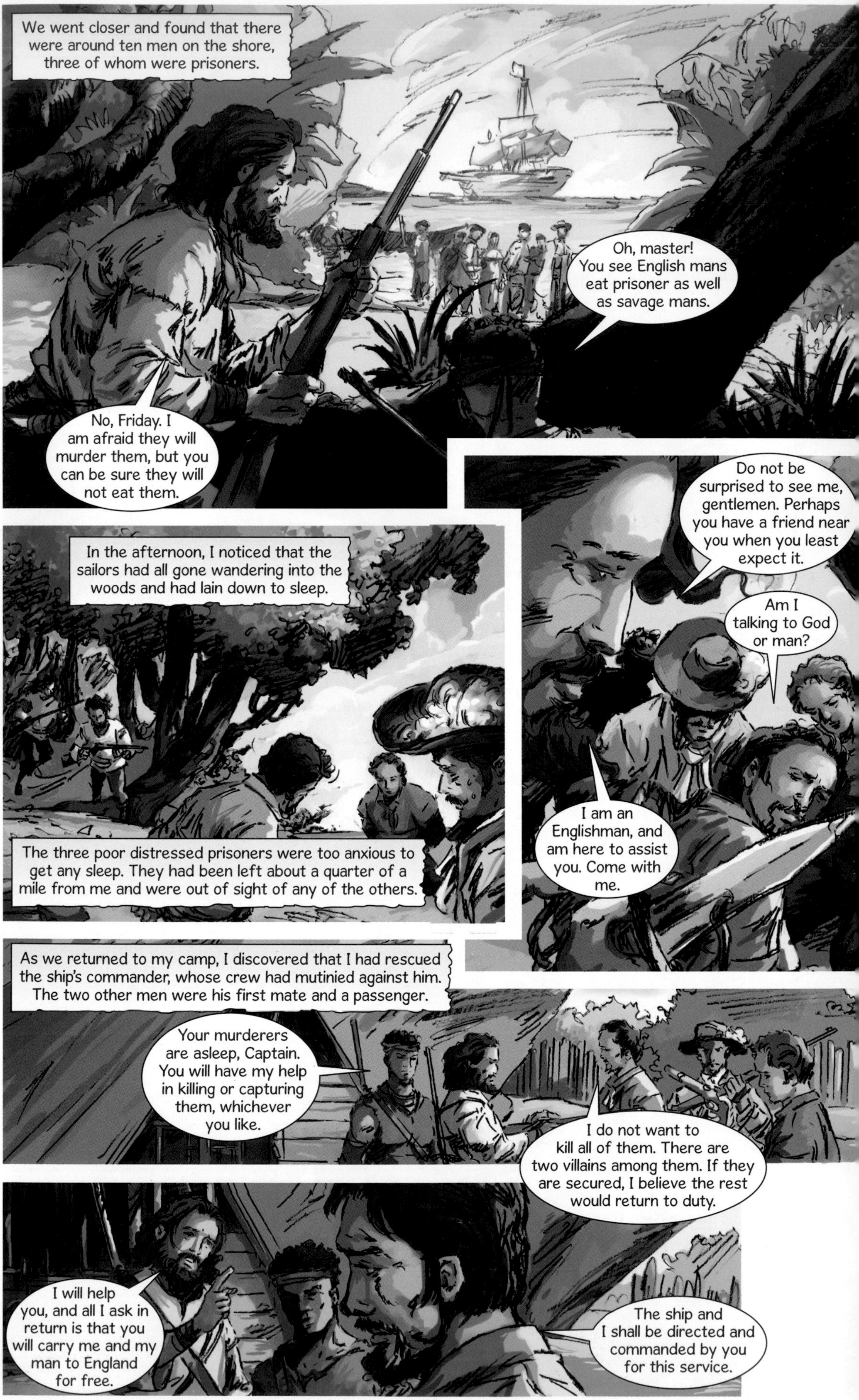
We went closer and found that there were around ten men on the shore, three of whom were prisoners.
Oh, master! You see English mans eat prisoner as well as savage mans.
No, Friday. I am afraid they will murder them, but you can be sure they will not eat them.
In the afternoon, I noticed that the sailors had all gone wandering into the woods and had lain down to sleep.
The three poor distressed prisoners were too anxious to get any sleep. They had been left about a quarter of a mile from me and were out of sight of any of the others.
Do not be surprised to see me, gentlemen. Perhaps you have a friend near you when you least expect it.
Am I talking to God or man?
I am an Englishman, and am here to assist you. Come with me.
As we returned to my camp, I discovered that I had rescued the ship's commander, whose crew had mutinied against him. The two other men were his first mate and a passenger.
Your murderers are asleep, Captain. You will have my help in killing or capturing them, whichever you like.
I do not want to kill all of them. There are two villains among them. If they are secured, I believe the rest would return to duty.
I will help you, and all I ask in return is that you will carry me and my man to England for free.
The ship and I shall be directed and commanded by you for this service.

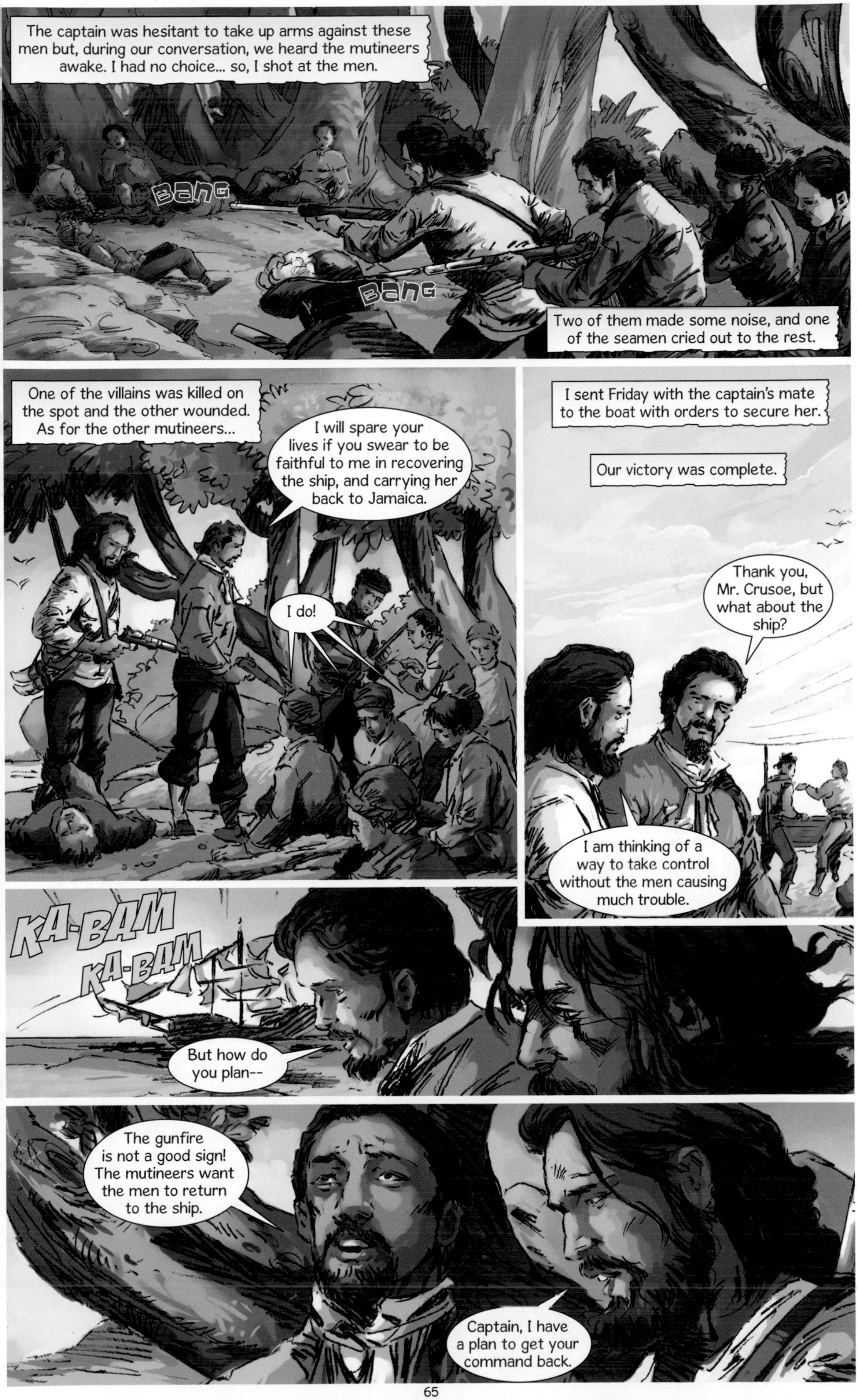
The captain was hesitant to take up arms against these men but, during our conversation, we heard the mutineers awake. I had no choice... so, I shot at the men.
BANG
BANG
Two of them made some noise, and one of the seamen cried out to the rest.
One of the villains was killed on the spot and the other wounded. As for the other mutineers...
I will spare your lives if you swear to be faithful to me in recovering the ship, and carrying her back to Jamaica.
I do!
I sent Friday with the captain's mate to the boat with orders to secure her.
Our victory was complete.
Thank you, Mr. Crusoe, but what about the ship?
I am thinking of a way to take control without the men causing much trouble.
KA-BAM
KA-BAM
But how do you plan--
The gunfire is not a good sign! The mutineers want the men to return to the ship.
Captain, I have a plan to get your command back.

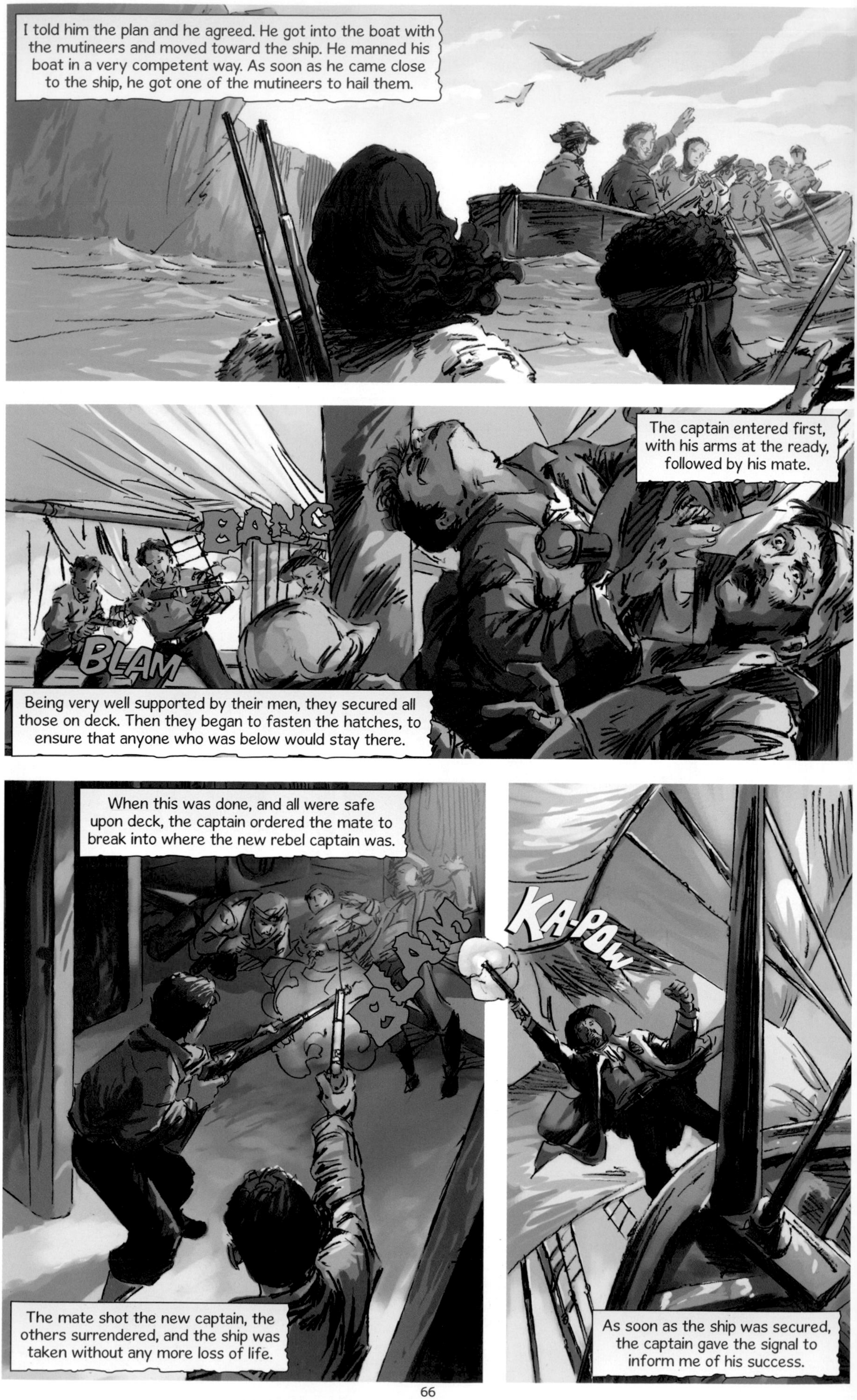

I told him the plan and he agreed. He got into the boat with the mutineers and moved toward the ship. He manned his boat in a very competent way. As soon as he came close to the ship, he got one of the mutineers to hail them.
The captain entered first, with his arms at the ready, followed by his mate.
BANG
BLAM
Being very well supported by their men, they secured all those on deck. Then they began to fasten the hatches, to ensure that anyone who was below would stay there.
When this was done, and all were safe upon deck, the captain ordered the mate to break into where the new rebel captain was.
BAM
The mate shot the new captain, the others surrendered, and the ship was taken without any more loss of life.
KA-POW
As soon as the ship was secured, the captain gave the signal to inform me of his success.

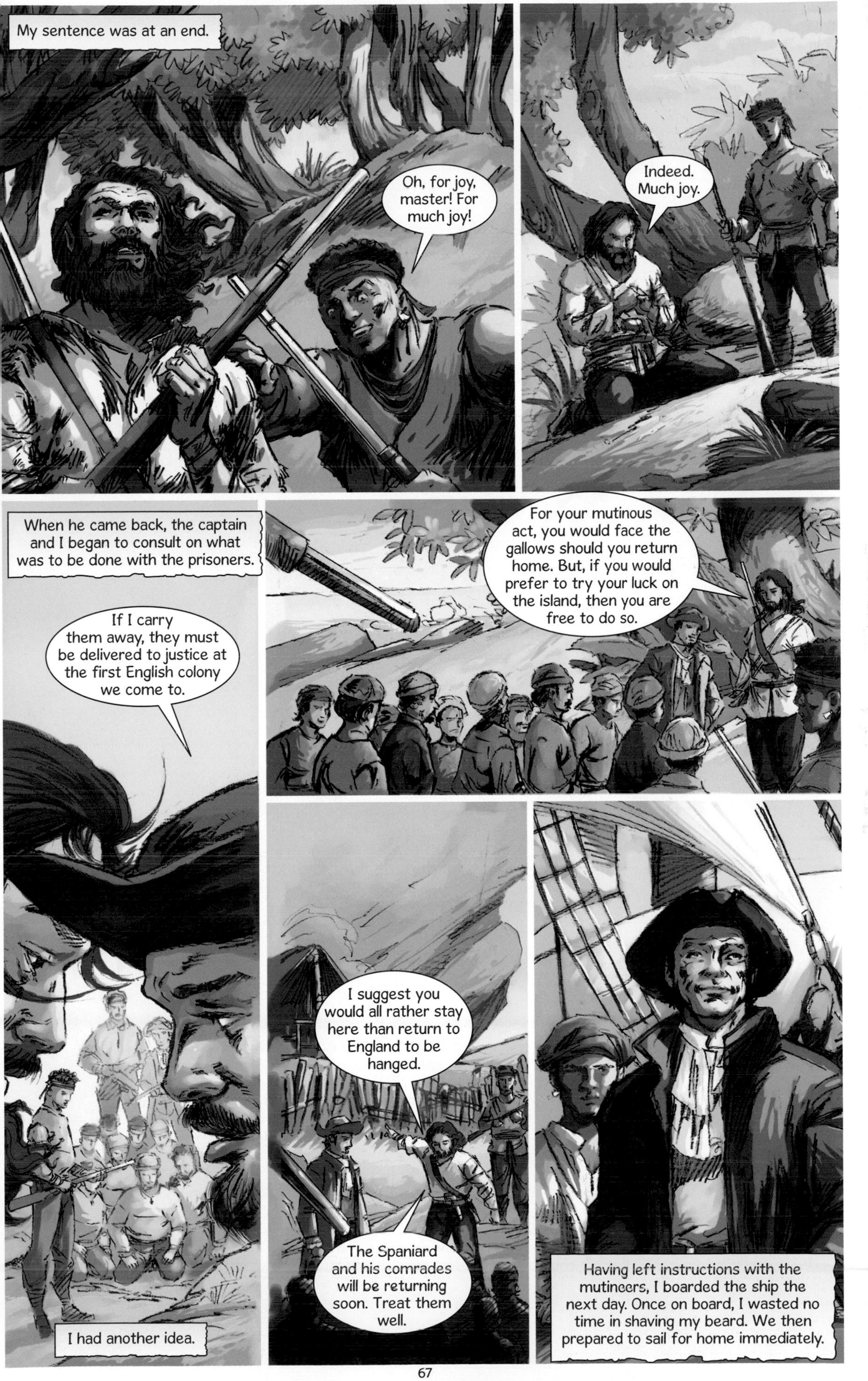
My sentence was at an end.
Oh, for joy, master! For much joy!
Indeed. Much joy.
When he came back, the captain and I began to consult on what was to be done with the prisoners.
If I carry them away, they must be delivered to justice at the first English colony we come to.
I had another idea.
For your mutinous act, you would face the gallows should you return home. But, if you would prefer to try your luck on the island, then you are free to do so.
I suggest you would all rather stay here than return to England to be hanged.
The Spaniard and his comrades will be returning soon. Treat them well.
Having left instructions with the mutineers, I boarded the ship the next day. Once on board, I wasted no time in shaving my beard. We then prepared to sail for home immediately.

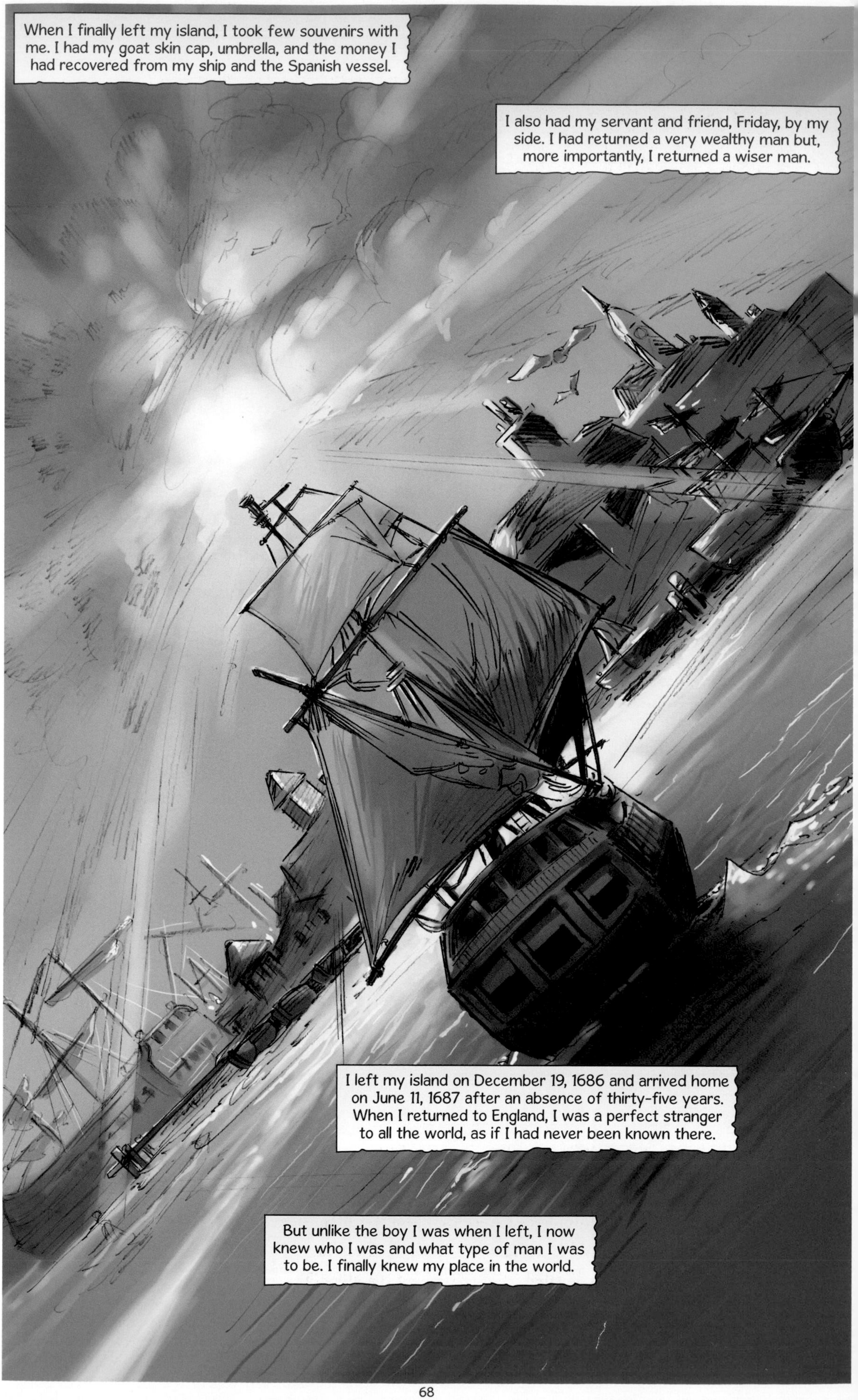
When I finally left my island, I took few souvenirs with me. I had my goat skin cap, umbrella, and the money I had recovered from my ship and the Spanish vessel.
I also had my servant and friend, Friday, by my side. I had returned a very wealthy man but, more importantly, I returned a wiser man.
I left my island on December 19, 1686 and arrived home on June 11, 1687 after an absence of thirty-five years. When I returned to England, I was a perfect stranger to all the world, as if I had never been known there.
But unlike the boy I was when I left, I now knew who I was and what type of man I was to be. I finally knew my place in the world.

Adventure Classics

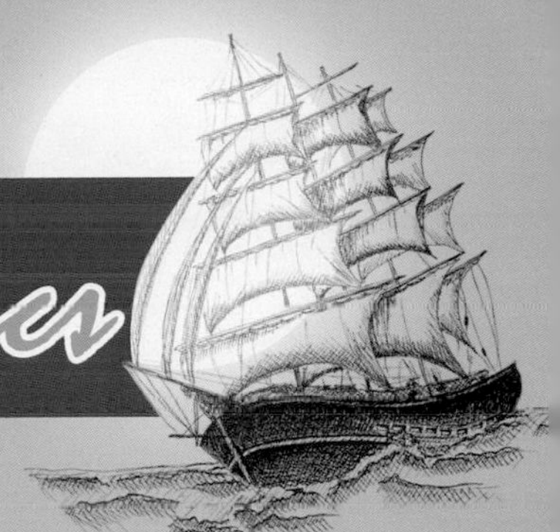

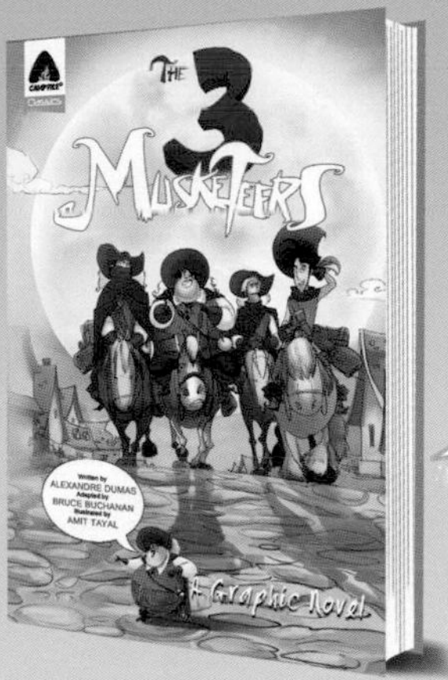
THE 3 MUSKETEERS
Written by ALEXANDRE DUMAS Adapted by BRUCE BUCHANAN Illustrated by AMIT TAYAL
A Graphic Novel

In a courtroom full of conspirators, the safety of France's King Lousie XIII and the honor of Queen Anne rest in the hands of d'Artagnan and his musketeer friends Athos, Porthos and Aramis. But with Cardinal Richelieu always a step ahead of them, will they succeed? A tale of dashing knights, beautiful ladies, conniving counts and above all... honor.

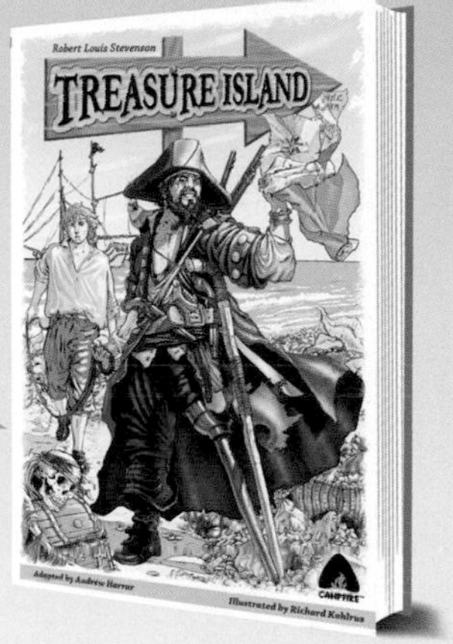
Robert Louis Stevenson
TREASURE ISLAND
Adapted by Andrew Harrar
Illustrated by Richard Kohlrus

When Jim finds sailor Billy Bones's secret map, his life takes a turn for the unexpected. The map holds the secret to the treasure of the notorious dead pirate—Captain Flint! And so begins Jim's journey of a lifetime as he sails the high seas in search of the buried treasure chest. But is the adventure worth the risk? Find out, in this exciting graphic novel adaptation!

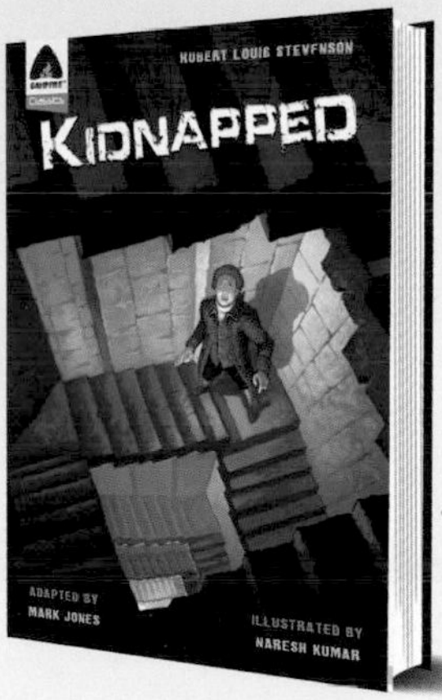
ROBERT LOUIS STEVENSON
KIDNAPPED
ADAPTED BY MARK JONES
ILLUSTRATED BY NARESH KUMAR

When David Balfour approaches his uncle Ebenezer to claim his inheritance, little is he aware of his uncle's plans for his future. Bound and gagged, David is left on a ship setting sail for the American Colonies. As he travels the wild highlands, he finds himself in the company of the revolutionary Jacobite Alan Breck. From artfully dodging Redcoats to playing the bagpipes, the duo will do anything to survive! But will they make it? Find out!

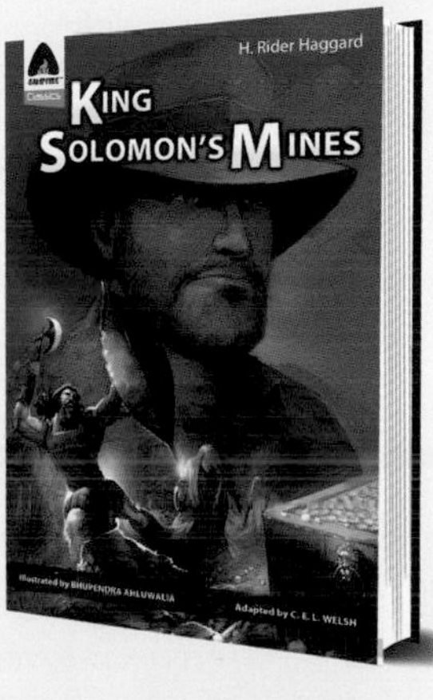
H. Rider Haggard
KING SOLOMON'S MINES
Illustrated by BHUPENDRA AHLUWALIA
Adapted by C. E. L. WELSH

In a land shrouded in mystery, three men set out in search of a lost man. Following the trail of Sir Henry Curtis's brother, Allan Quatermain and his team, including the regal Umbopa, find themselves on a path that may lead them to a king's treasure! But with a vengeful king as their host and an evil witch plotting against them, chances for success look slim. Experience their journey as they fight fierce tribes and sorcery in the depths of the African continent!

FIVE FAMOUS SHIPWRECKS

MARY ROSE

Once described by Henry VIII as 'the fairest flower of all the ships that ever sailed', the *Mary Rose* took two years to build and was fitted with a 'broadside'. This meant that its cannons were placed on one side of the ship, providing devastating fire power against enemy vessels. On July 19, 1545, the *Mary Rose* keeled over as it sailed out to engage French ships in battle. An exact explanation of why the ship sank has yet to be found, but it is thought that over 600 crew members died that day. When the *Mary Rose* wreck was lifted from the sea in 1982, the event was captured by television cameras and watched by an estimated 60 million viewers.

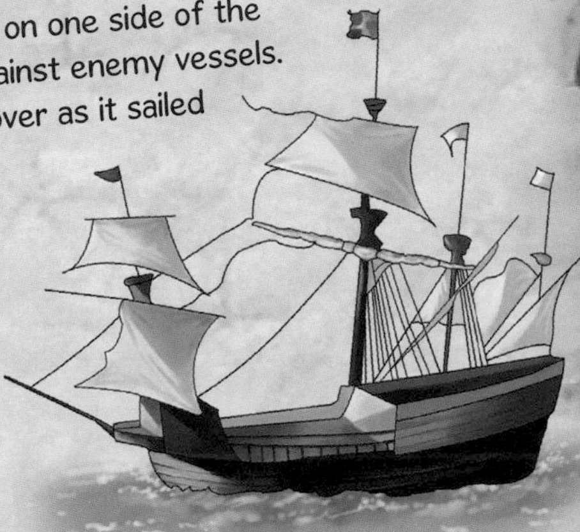

TITANIC

The *Titanic* was the most extravagant passenger liner of her era, meant to be completely unsinkable. Wealthy travelers could enjoy the use of an on-board swimming pool, an extensive library, a gym, and a Turkish bath. After colliding with an iceberg on April 15, 1912, the *Titanic* sank into the North Atlantic Ocean on its maiden voyage from Southampton to New York. The resting place of the *Titanic* is 2.5 miles underwater.

There were suggestions of a *Titanic* curse due to the presence of the mummy of Princess of Amen-Ra on board. The owner of the mummy took it onto the ship hidden under his car to avoid causing a panic among the passengers.

There are striking similarities between the novel *Futility* by M. F. Mansfield and the real-life story of the *Titanic*. The amazing fact is that the novel was first published in 1898—fourteen years before the *Titanic* sank!!

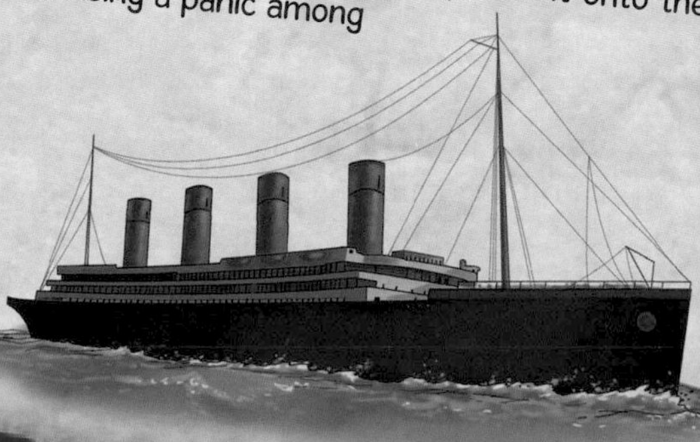

LUSITANIA

Built to be a British passenger liner, the *Lusitania* was handed over to the British Admiralty and equipped with twelve 6-inch guns in August 1914. This was due to the outbreak of the First World War. A German embassy later issued a warning notice in American newspapers to travelers. It stated that a war existed between Germany and Britain, and that the waters adjacent to the British Isles were considered a war zone. It stated that travelers sailing there do so at their own risk. On Friday, May 9, 1915, the *Lusitania* was sunk by a torpedo from a U20 German submarine. One of the casualties was Justus Miles Forman, an American novelist and playwright. It is strange that days before he embarked on the *Lusitania* voyage, he received a mysterious phone call which warned him not to board it.

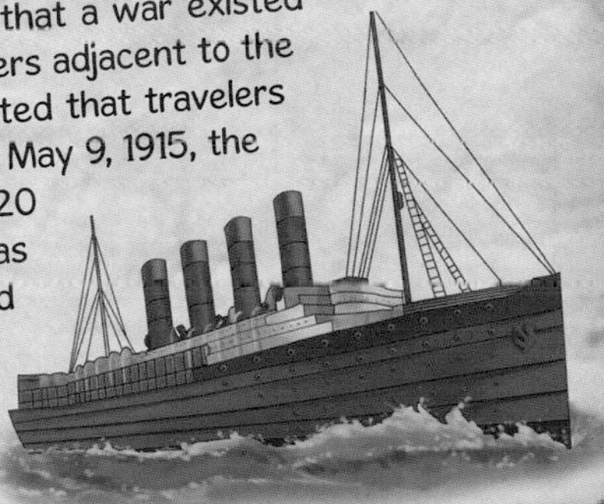

BISMARCK

An intimidating German warship, the *Bismarck* had a displacement of 50,000 tons, a top speed of 30 knots, was 17-storeys high, and over 800-feet long. During the Second World War, the British Prime Minister, Winston Churchill, gave orders for the *Bismarck* to be sunk on sight. In May 1941, the *Bismarck* was chased by the British navy for 8 days. Faced with such a bombardment, the ship was heavily damaged, and sank. In 1989, after searching an area of 200 square miles, Dr. Robert D. Ballard found the wreck of the *Bismarck*—it was more than 15,000 feet beneath the surface of the Atlantic!

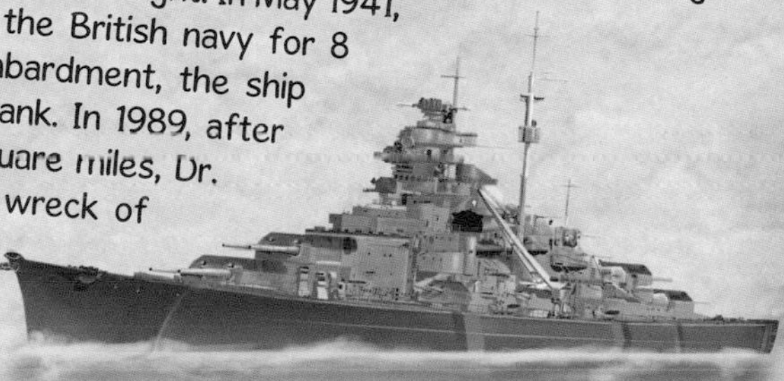

BELGRANO

On May 2, 1982, an Argentine Navy cruiser known as the *Belgrano* was attacked by *HMS Conqueror*, the British nuclear submarine. Three torpedoes were fired at the Argentine warship, which sank as a result of the damage. The *Belgrano* had previously been an American ship which had survived the Japanese attack on Pearl Harbor during the Second World War. The ship was sold to Argentina during the 1950s. In 2003, a film company attempted to search for the ship using a remote-controlled submersible, and sonar equipment. The crew did not manage to find the wreck, which is thought to be 180 kilometers off the coast of Argentina, known for its dangerous seas.

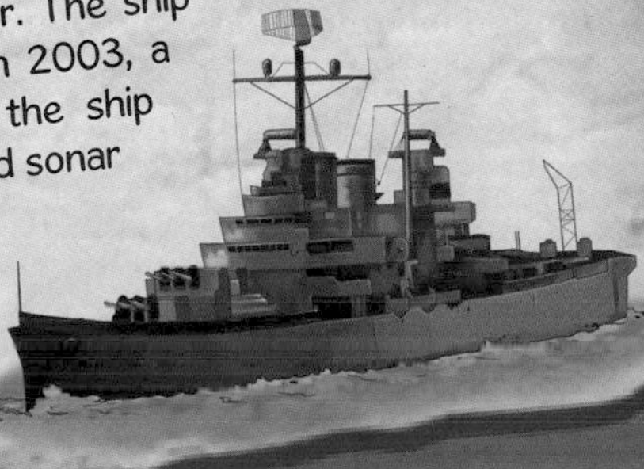

You may also like to read other titles from our

Classics Series

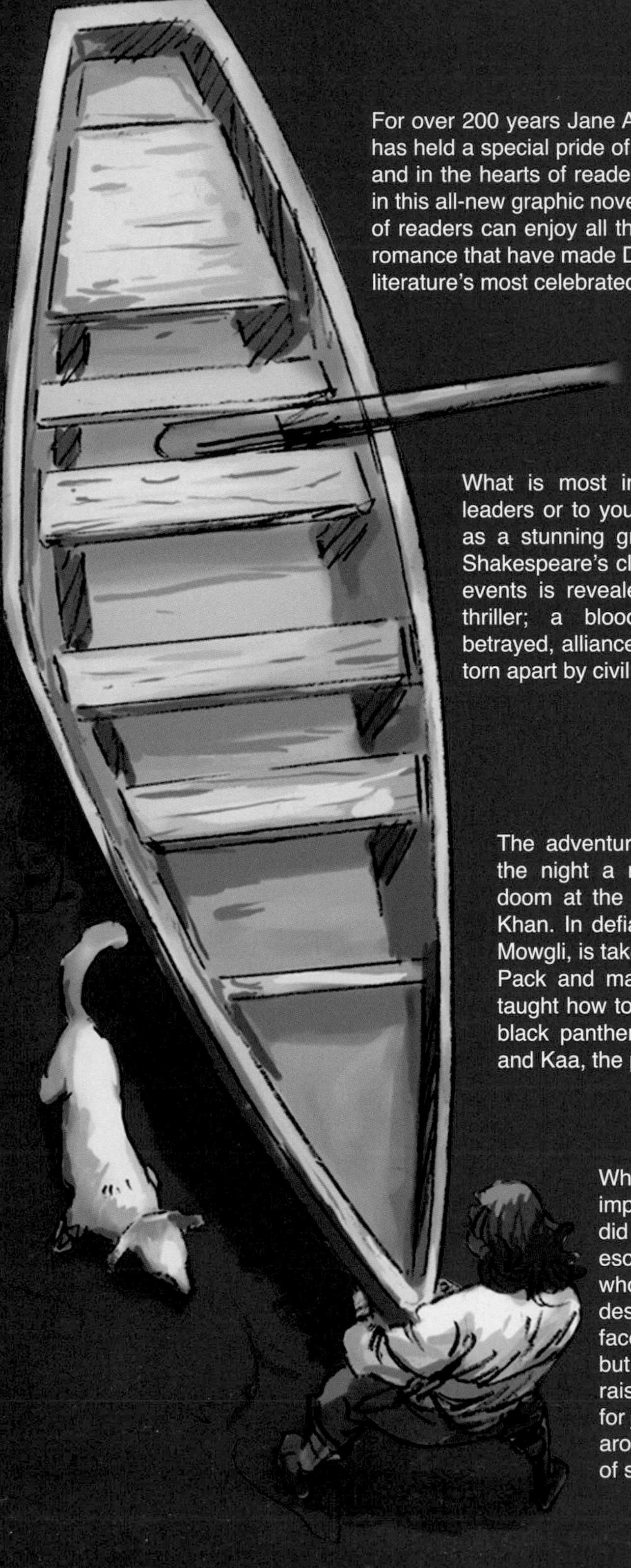

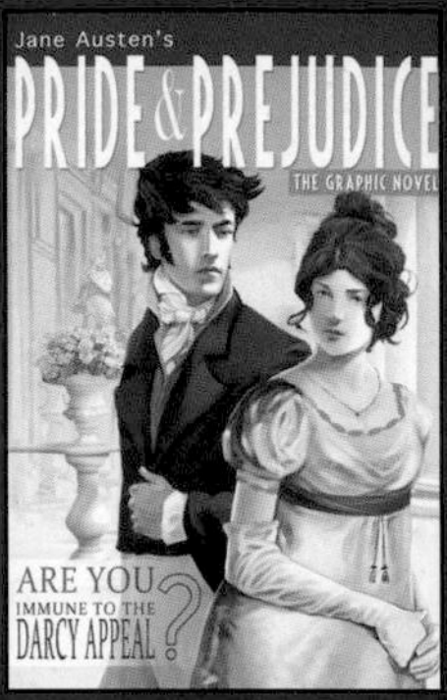
Jane Austen's
PRIDE & PREJUDICE
THE GRAPHIC NOVEL
ARE YOU IMMUNE TO THE DARCY APPEAL?

For over 200 years Jane Austen's *Pride & Prejudice* has held a special pride of place on the bookshelves and in the hearts of readers around the world. Now, in this all-new graphic novel format a new generation of readers can enjoy all the comedy, heartache and romance that have made Darcy and Elizabeth one of literature's most celebrated couples.

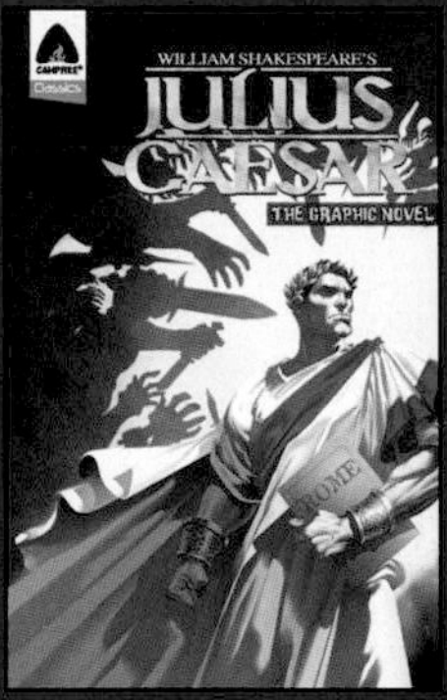
WILLIAM SHAKESPEARE'S
JULIUS CAESAR
THE GRAPHIC NOVEL
ROME

What is most important, loyalty to your leaders or to your country? Now imagined as a stunning graphic adventure, William Shakespeare's classic retelling of historical events is revealed as a timeless political thriller; a bloody saga of friendships betrayed, alliances destroyed, and a nation torn apart by civil war.

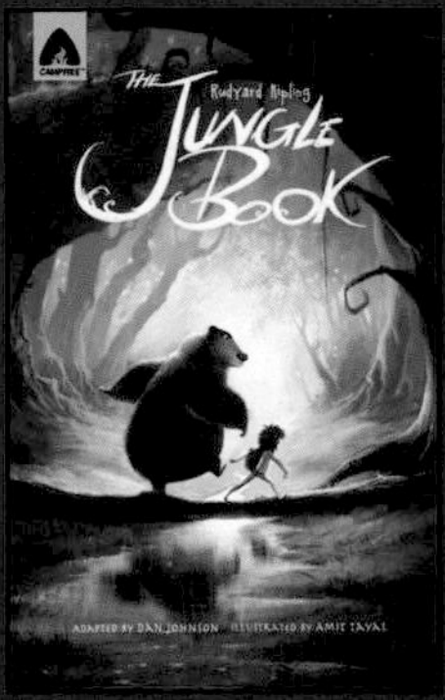
Rudyard Kipling
THE JUNGLE BOOK

The adventure of a lifetime begins on the night a man-cub escapes certain doom at the hands of the tiger Shere Khan. In defiance of the tiger, the boy, Mowgli, is taken in by the Seeonee Wolf Pack and made a member. Mowgli is taught how to survive by Bagheera, the black panther; Baloo, the brown bear; and Kaa, the python.

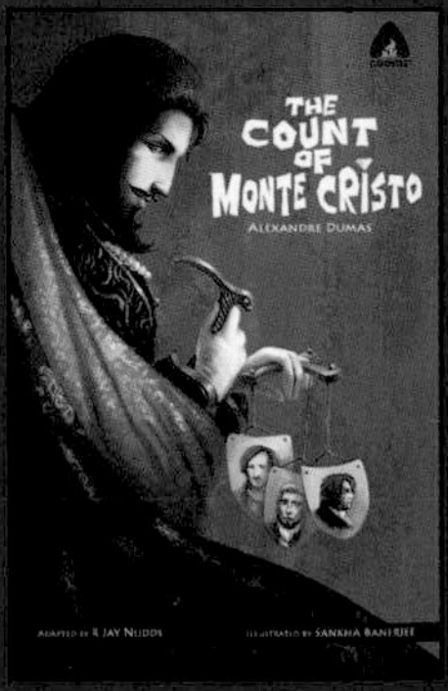
THE COUNT OF MONTE CRISTO
ALEXANDRE DUMAS

When Edmond Dantès is imprisoned for a crime he did not commit, he vows to escape and destroy those who betrayed him. Acting as destiny's agent, Dantès must face not only his enemies, but also the moral dilemmas raised by his ruthless quest for justice. Manipulating those around him, he leaves a trail of social carnage in his wake.